Praise for The Highlander's Christmas Countess:

"A witty, charming romance, the perfect Christmas gift!" **Christine Wells, bestselling author of Sisters of the Resistance**

"Lose yourself in the Highlands with Anna Campbell's Lairds Most Likely. You won't be disappointed." **Annie West, USA Today bestselling author**

"If you are looking for a quick, enjoyable holiday read, then I would definitely pick this one up!" **Historical Romance Lover**

"This delightful story is guaranteed to bring some warmth and Christmas cheer during the holiday season." **Roses Are Blue Reviews**

"Filled with family, friends, love, and romance, *The Highlander's Christmas Countess* was a perfect read for the holidays. I had adored the romance between Hamish and Emily and it was lovely to see them again. I enjoyed watching Quentin as he investigated his suspicions and finally dismantled Kit's disguise. Even better was Kit's willingness to open up to Quentin and share her problems for them to solve together. I simply adored their story." **Kathy's Review Corner**

"It was such tender, sweet wooing on Quentin's part in how he gained Kit's trust. He did through care, tenderness, and humor. I loved how the author handled the lovely, passionate, and slow build to the consummation of their marriage." **Amazon Review**

"Definitely a Christmas novella to reread every year." *5 stars Amazon Review*

"Despite this only being novella length, the characters jumped out of the page and were more well-rounded than a lot of characters in many of the full length novels I've read recently. The romance was just lovely and sweet and I went away feeling like this couple would have a proper, realistic happily ever after." *GoodReads Review*

"This is an ideal read with a cuppa tea and your favorite reading snacks, a fire and your favorite reading chair. You can never go wrong with a book by Ms. Campbell. Enjoy!!" *5 stars GoodReads Review*

"Anna has given another delightful read with characters that draw you in and make you fall in love just as they do." *5 stars GoodReads Review*

ALSO BY ANNA CAMPBELL

Claiming the Courtesan

Untouched

Tempt the Devil

Captive of Sin

My Reckless Surrender

Midnight's Wild Passion

The Sons of Sin Series:

Seven Nights in a Rogue's Bed

Days of Rakes and Roses

A Rake's Midnight Kiss

What a Duke Dares

A Scoundrel by Moonlight

Three Proposals and a Scandal

The Dashing Widows Series:

The Seduction of Lord Stone

Tempting Mr. Townsend

Winning Lord West

Pursuing Lord Pascal

Charming Sir Charles

Catching Captain Nash

Lord Garson's Bride

The Lairds Most Likely Series:

The Laird's Willful Lass

The Laird's Christmas Kiss

The Highlander's Lost Lady

The Highlander's Defiant Captive

The Highlander's Christmas Quest

The Highlander's English Bride

The Highlander's Forbidden Mistress

The Highlander's Christmas Countess

The Highlander's Rescued Maiden

The Highlander's Christmas Lassie

A Scandal in Mayfair Series:

One Wicked Wish

Two Secret Sins

Three Times Tempted

Christmas Stories:

The Winter Wife

Her Christmas Earl

A Pirate for Christmas

Mistletoe and the Major

A Match Made in Mistletoe

The Christmas Stranger

His Christmas Cinderella (in the anthology A Grosvenor Square Christmas)

Other Books:

These Haunted Hearts

Stranded with the Scottish Earl

The Highlander's Christmas Countess

The Lairds Most Likely Book 8

ANNA CAMPBELL

To my dear friend Sally Horton! I promised I'd
dedicate a book to you one day and I always think
of you when I think of the Highlands.

CHAPTER ONE

Glen Lyon, Western Highlands of Scotland, 20th December 1830

"*K*it! Kit! Let's do it again!"

The imperious voice of five-year-old Miss Andromeda Douglas rose above the laughter and chatter echoing around the snowy glen.

"No, Kit! It's my turn! Come down the hill with me, Kit!" Master William Douglas, a year younger than his sister, demanded.

A light laugh and a cheerful voice responded. "He's right, Miss Andy. It is his turn. Ye can ride down with Uncle Joseph, if you're in such an all-fired hurry."

"But I want to go with you," the daughter of the house insisted, scorning the idea of accepting Joseph Laing, the head groom, as a substitute.

"In that case, you'll have to wait."

With a mince pie in his hand and a smile that he hoped hid his raging curiosity, Quentin MacNab turned to his Aunt Emily who stood beside him. "The new stable lad seems to be a favorite with the bairns."

A group consisting of the laird and lady and the senior members of the household gathered on the snowy slopes behind Lyon House. Beside them stretched a trestle table, laden with seasonal treats. The day was fine but bitterly cold. Perfect sledding weather.

Quentin had already taken the dizzying ride down the hill several times and had only drawn aside now to join his aunt and uncle in a mug of mulled wine. The scents of cinnamon and cloves lent a spicy note to the clean Highland air.

Emily Douglas smiled back. The Lady of Glen Lyon was a bonny woman, with rich dark brown hair and gray eyes that sparkled with intelligence. Despite being Quentin's aunt, she was only eight years older than his twenty-four. More friend than aunt.

"Yes, he's proven himself a treasure in this last month. Laing speaks highly of his work and as you can see, the children adore him. We were lucky Laing asked his nephew to come and work for us."

Quentin's gaze locked on the slim figure settling in behind the rambunctious heir to Glen Lyon. The stable lad seemed to have cut off Andy's tantrum before it could start, which spoke volumes for his tact and intelligence. "He's very well spoken for a stableboy."

Uncle Hamish turned, a slab of fruitcake in his massive hand. "Aye, apparently the lad was a favorite back in his village, too. When Kit wasn't busy on the family croft, the minister gave him lessons."

Uncle Hamish sounded as English as his wife, the result of a childhood spent in London. He was fair and brawny like a Viking, and while Quentin at six foot one was no midget, his uncle towered over him.

Quentin took a mouthful of his wine, appreciating the warmth. "Odd he aims no higher than a place in the stables, then. If he has a good education, he could find a post as a clerk somewhere or a teacher."

Quentin watched as the sled careered down the snowy slope. William's shrieks of delight filled the air, and the stableboy's face was bright with childlike excitement.

When Quentin turned back to Hamish and Emily, he caught them sharing a meaningful glance. That was nothing new. Quentin had lived at Glen Lyon for the last six months. He'd become used to silent communication between the laird and his lady.

Emily answered. "Kit's a genius with the horses and seems happiest working outdoors. I believe Laing is hoping that his nephew might take over as head groom after he retires."

"Although that won't be for years yet," Hamish added, before he took a bite of his fruit cake.

"Hmm." Quentin continued to observe the stable lad and the two children, the boy dark and intense and the girl as golden fair as her papa.

Speaking of family resemblances, Kit didn't look much like his uncle Joseph Laing. Quentin's gaze flickered toward the redheaded giant standing under the trees with the horses and wagons that had transported the sleds and the furniture for this alfresco winter party.

Kit and William reached the base of the hill and clambered off the sled. Holding William's hand, the stable lad started to haul the sled back up the hill. Andy bounced around on top of the slope, urging them to hurry.

Andy was a clever, outspoken lassie, very like her father in personality, too. Hamish Douglas, Laird of Glen Lyon, was a famous astronomer. Emily was hardly less distinguished in scientific circles. Quentin had come to Glen Lyon from his father's estate near Perth to work as his uncle's assistant. Hamish's older sister Prudence had suggested that her son might enjoy some time on the west coast with his uncle and aunt.

His mother had been right, as usual. Quentin was enjoying it. He loved Hamish and Emily and the children. He loved the elegant house on the shore of its sheltered sea loch. He loved the challenging work, although he was the first to admit that while he might be clever, he was nowhere near as clever as his brilliant uncle.

But as he watched Kit trudge up the hill toward Andy, he had to admit that by far the most interesting thing on the Glen Lyon estate was the laird's new stableboy. Thick trousers covered long legs – the lad gave the promise of height to come. A bulky, roughly woven coat fell from neck to knee, and a tight knitted bonnet covered his head and ears. In fact, the boy was considerably more bundled up than anyone else out here on this cold day, including the two children.

Quentin set his silver mug on the table. "I might go back to the sledding. If William will accept me in place of Kit, I might even take him with me."

Another of those speaking looks between his aunt and uncle. "Kit has it all in hand," Hamish said with a hint of disapproval.

"No doubt," Quentin said and strode up the hill to Kit and the two children.

"It's my turn now," Andy was saying, as dictatorial as any princess. "You have to wait, William."

"Now, Miss Andy, there's nae need to rub it in," Kit said, a gurgle of laughter adding a rich edge of warmth to the gentle reprimand.

"I've got a better idea," Quentin said, with a shaming hint of breathlessness. That hill was deuced steep. It was a lot easier coming down it on a sled than climbing it on two legs. "I'll take William."

"Oh, Cousin Quentin, yes, please, yes, please!" the child shrieked, jumping up and down with excitement.

Two large bluebell-colored eyes surrounded by thick black lashes fixed on Quentin with a hint of wariness. The cold weather had put pink in Kit's cheeks. He was a delicate-looking creature to be working somewhere as rough-and-tumble as the stables. This close, Quentin could see that the body under all that heavy clothing was slight.

"Aye, sir." Kit bowed, before sidling away. "He'll love that."

Quentin had already noticed that the lad was painfully shy and inclined to avoid company other than the children. A few times, he'd set out to talk to Kit, only to turn around and find the lad had scarpered out of sight.

He waved a hand through the air. "No, stay."

"Aye, sir." But reluctance weighted the obedience, Quentin could hear.

He held that bright blue gaze until the pink in the stable lad's cheeks turned vivid. The boy's glance flickered away, and he seemed flustered as he placed Andy on the sled and positioned himself behind the little girl.

"Let's go," Andy commanded.

"Aye," Kit said, the husky tone sending a jolt of awareness through Quentin. His hands closed into fists at his sides, and his nostrils flared. He knew now how a hound felt when it scented a fox.

William tugged at his sleeve, and he started as if he woke from a dream. "Cousin Quentin, can we go, too?"

"Aye." He looked down at the little boy and smiled. "I'll just give Kit and Andy a push."

"Nae need, sir," the stable lad said, then released a surprised "Oh!" as Quentin ignored that and the sled began to slide downward.

The sledding went on until the short day drew to a close. As the hours passed, the stableboy's nervousness faded, Quentin noticed. But then, after asking Kit to stay, he'd done his best to conceal his avid curiosity. He also noted that as far as possible in the circumstances, which wasn't very far at all, the lad kept his distance and ducked his head to avoid any searching looks.

Eventually William tired, but Andy remained as greedy for thrills as ever. "Just one more time, Kit. Please."

"Kit's done enough," Emily said. She'd climbed the hill to gather her offspring and usher them down to the cart for the ride home.

"I'm sure I can manage one more, my lady," the boy said.

"She'll keep you here all night if she can," Quentin said.

"Aye, sir," the boy said, sticking to the monosyllabic responses he'd supplied most of the afternoon.

"Please, Mamma, just one more," Andy wheedled.

Emily gave a longsuffering sigh. "You're a little horror, Andromeda Mary Douglas."

"Och, the lassie just has high spirits," Kit said.

"Doesn't she just?" Emily cast the stableboy a laughing glance. "Are you up for one more go, Kit?

You've been marvelous with them, but you've done more than your share."

"Aye, my lady."

"Goody," Andy said, plopping herself down on the sled with a smug expression.

"I'll give you a push," Quentin said, as Kit took a protective position behind the gilt-haired little girl.

"Hold on tight, Miss Andy," Kit said, then couldn't contain a shriek of excitement as the sled gathered speed down the hill.

The shriek turned into a cry of panic, as the sled hit some invisible barrier and shot up into the air. Its two occupants went flying.

Time slowed to a standstill as Quentin watched in horror. Then, with dread cramping his gut, he broke into a run toward Kit and Andy.

"Andy!" Emily cried, also scrambling down the hill toward the two bodies sprawled over the snow.

Quentin was just ahead of her. He rushed past Andy, who already sat up, to where the lad lay unmoving. Terror tasting rusty on his tongue, he fell to his knees at Kit's side. Shaking hands helped him to turn over. The knitted hat had come off in the fall, revealing an untidy mop of unevenly cropped black hair.

"Kit! Are you all right? Can you move? Where does it hurt?"

Quentin's hold was gentle, as he cradled Kit against his chest. The boy smelled not unpleasantly of the stables. Horses and fresh sweat and hay, and beneath that an incongruous hint of flowers.

Kit looked pale and shocked, and the slender body in his arms was trembling. Those extraordinary eyes turned up to his face then darted away. The force of that charged blue gaze struck Quentin like a blow. His concerned questions jammed in his tightening throat.

"Mamma, that was fun," Andy informed her frantic mother.

"Dreadful child," Emily said, her voice thick with the remnants of fear as she hugged her daughter.

"Is she all right?" Hamish asked, rushing up.

"It would take a cannon to put a dent in this one," Emily said. She turned to where Quentin had dragged Kit out of the snowdrift. "What about Kit?"

He cleared his throat and made himself look away from Kit's face. "I think he's fine."

"I'm...I'm unharmed, my lady," Kit said, trying to push away from Quentin, but too shaken after the accident to make much of a job of it. He fumbled after his lost hat.

Quentin located the hat and passed it over, noticing how quickly the boy tugged it down around his ears and low to his uncompromising dark eyebrows. "Can you sit up?"

"Aye, I'm sure I can," Kit said in a muffled voice, although he remained still and he kept his head down. "How is Miss Andy?"

"Her parents are with her. She seems her usual self, not even frightened. You're the one I'm worried about."

"I've suffered nae damage, thank ye, sir. I think you should leave me and go and tend to the bairn," the lad said with an incongruous touch of hauteur. "I'm but a servant, after all."

"We're all equal in God's eyes," Quentin said piously.

Kit rewarded him with a flash of annoyance that made him want to smile. It became clear that the lad might be bruised, but otherwise he was in one piece.

There was no excuse to keep holding onto Kit. But it was only with the greatest reluctance that he released the stableboy. Quentin's thoughts were in a tumult. The moment he'd touched that slim form, he'd confirmed his long-held suspicions. Although now he knew for sure, a thousand questions badgered him.

This wasn't the time to ask them, when Kit had had an accident and even worse, regarded him with crushed bluebell eyes, bright with apprehension.

"Can we do it again?" Andy was asking her mother. "That was like flying."

"No, you cannot, you dreadful little miss," her mother said, laughing. "And don't you want to know if Kit is all right?"

"He's with Quentin. People are always all right with Quentin," the child said, with all the certainty of a five-year-old who knew everything there was to know.

Quentin arched one brow at the slight, boyish figure gingerly shifting to sit up under his own powers in the snow. He hoped to tease out more of that intriguing impudence. "High praise indeed."

But the stable lad had repented of his brief insurrection and stared back with a stony expression. "As you say, sir."

Hamish rose from where he kneeled near his daughter and strode toward them. "Come away inside, Kit and Quentin. It's getting cold and dark. Kit, are you hurt?"

"I'm gey sure I'm no', Douglas," the lad said in a gruffer voice than Quentin had heard from him all afternoon. And with a stronger Scottish accent. Quentin had already noticed that the Highland burr in the lad's speech was an unreliable visitor.

"Here, let me help you up."

Quentin noticed Kit's relieved expression as Hamish heaved him to his feet. They were attracting a crowd. Emily bustled over with Andy in tow, while

William and Laing scrambled down the hill toward them. When William stumbled with tiredness as they approached, Laing picked him up and gave him a few encouraging words.

"Are ye in one piece, nephew?" Laing asked, once he was within earshot.

"Never better, Uncle," Kit said.

"What a bouncer," Quentin protested. "You must be black and blue after that tumble."

The look that the boy shot him conveyed dislike – before the obedient servant expression descended again. "No real harm was done, sir," Kit said in a wooden tone.

"Nonetheless, it was a nasty wee spill," Laing said to his nephew. "Ye can sit up with me when we go back to the house."

"Thank you, Uncle," Kit said and turned to collect the sled from where it had landed upside down in the snow.

Quentin rushed to take it from the stable lad. "Go and sit on the cart. Nobody expects you to help pack up." He hadn't missed the way movement had made Kit hide a wince. "I think we should get the doctor in."

Huge eyes fastened on him with horror. "No!"

Kit's hands clenched on the sled. Just before fighting over the sled turned into a wrestle, the lad surrendered. He dropped his head and mumbled, "Thank ye for your concern, Mr. MacNab. I'm just a wee bit knocked about. My uncle has some liniment that will have me right as rain tomorrow."

"Liniment for horses," Quentin said, knowing that Kit wished him to Hades for his fussing.

Yet again, the lad didn't meet his eyes. "We are all creatures under God's eyes, I believe, sir."

As Quentin burst into laughter, Kit turned away and moved with surprising speed toward the cart.

After supper in the servants' hall, a meal enlivened by excitement about the looming Christmas celebrations, Kit slipped away from the cozy big house to the scarcely less cozy stables. At Glen Lyon, the horses lived in luxury. But then the estate was a good example of just how to manage a property. All the crofters' cottages were in good repair, fencing and equipment were in fine fettle, nobody complained under Hamish and Emily Douglas's authority. At the last place Kit had been, things hadn't been nearly so well-run.

Aching from the aftereffects of his accident, he climbed the stairs to the room he'd been given near the head groom's apartment. Because of his privileged position as Laing's nephew, he didn't have to share his quarters with anyone else.

Kit entered the room and bolted the door behind him. With a weary sigh, he sank against the door. He was sore and bruised, and his adventures with the runaway sled had roused far too much interest at dinner. Not to mention that Quentin MacNab's kindness after the spill had left him thoroughly unsettled.

Quentin MacNab, handsome as the devil, with his thick, tawny hair and sharp hazel eyes that never missed a trick. Since Hamish's nephew had evinced an interest in the new stableboy, Kit had done his best to stay out of the way. But today's exploits had placed him firmly in Mr. MacNab's sights, plague take it.

With another sigh, Kit straightened and stepped into the middle of the floor to undress. First to come off was the thick coat, followed by the woolen jerkin and the linen shirt. Then, very carefully, he unwound the binding that constricted his chest, swearing under his breath as he noted the purple marks blossoming over his white skin.

And just like that, Kit Laing became Christabel Urquhart.

CHAPTER TWO

*A*long with most of the Glen Lyon household, Kit set out on the next afternoon's expedition to gather greenery to decorate the house for the festive season. As they did most years, the laird and his lady were hosting a big house party for Christmas, and the guests were due to start arriving on Christmas Eve for a gala ball.

Kit had heard so many tales below stairs of an event brimming with glamour and fun. Because Emily was English and Hamish had spent most of his childhood in London, Christmas at Glen Lyon was a joyous mixture of traditions, unlike anything Kit had ever experienced before. The guests stayed over until Boxing Day, then there was a huge ceilidh that night for the servants and the crofters, where jigs and reels were more likely to feature than fashionable waltzes and quadrilles.

Kit looked forward to being part of that. The servants at Glen Lyon were a contented lot and had given her a warm welcome when she arrived a month ago, ostensibly as Joseph Laing's nephew. There had been some mild grumbling from the other junior grooms, when she received the privilege of a room to herself, but Laing had jumped on that straightaway and scotched the trouble at the source.

That private room had helped her to maintain her disguise, and she'd done her best to avoid too much notice while she worked. Until yesterday, when an overturned sled had nearly brought her to grief.

After those dramas, she intended to keep her head down during this visit to the woods that grew up behind the house and spread over into the next glen. She'd already noticed Mr. MacNab looking at her in a way that made her fear he might have guessed that she wasn't what she appeared.

Kit blushed to recall his gentle, efficient hands on her when he'd dug her out of the snowdrift. He'd never touched her before and when he did, it had been difficult to remember that she was a stableboy and not a young lady. Not to mention a young lady who had noted from the first how handsome the MacNab heir was.

Hamish Douglas, the laird, was also handsome, but somehow he was a little too much the king of the beasts to make Kit's heart beat faster. Which was a good thing when Hamish was besotted with his wife.

But Quentin MacNab? Now there was a fine figure of a man.

Tall and lean and with a mass of untidy honey-brown hair. More, he was always ready with a laugh and an encouraging word, and she noticed how good he was with the children and the servants and the horses. All of that spoke to a good heart. He was clever, too, but not enough to overawe her. A contented man, easy in his rangy, elegant body. A man who looked at advantage on a horse or striding across the wild hills around Glen Lyon.

Kit already had more problems than she could count. She shouldn't waste her time mooning over the laird's nephew. But she couldn't help it. He seemed such a perfect example of his sex.

After yesterday, she knew he had hazel eyes, a fascinating mixture of green and gold. Until the sledding accident, she hadn't ventured close enough to discover that. When those eyes had stared directly at her, they'd set her heart racing with very un-servant-like excitement.

But Mr. MacNab had seen too much yesterday, and wisdom dictated that if she wished to preserve her disguise, she should stay out of his way. Every instinct insisted that she could trust him, but for the moment, it was safer to maintain the illusion that she was Kit Laing, stableboy extraordinaire.

Which made it irritating in the extreme that so far today, Mr. MacNab had dogged her footsteps. Andy and William had followed her about since she'd arrived. She now discovered the completely different effect of a six-foot-tall man doing the same thing.

"Kit, will you carry me?" Andy whined from behind her. For once, William wasn't trailing Kit. Instead, he was over with the grooms, making a mess of stacking some pine cones. "I'm tired."

Now Kit hid a groan and summoned a smile for the little girl. Kit was stiff from yesterday's mishap with the sled. Today, hauling the laird's daughter about was too much to ask.

"I willnae carry you, Miss Andy. I'll give ye a ride on the handcart. That will be fun."

"It would be more fun if you carry me." A mutinous expression settled on the fairylike face as happy laughter and shouting echoed from the woods around them.

Miss Andromeda Douglas promised to grow up to become a hoyden, Kit thought, and liked her the better for it. She only wished that she'd managed to find her own spirit earlier. It might have changed the way things had played out.

Or perhaps not.

"What is it, Kit?" Mr. MacNab asked from a few feet away. Despite her best efforts, she hadn't been able to shake him. "Are you still sore from yesterday?"

She plastered a smile on her face, and cursed those penetrating hazel eyes, however much they might make her traitorous heart skip. "No, sir. But thank ye for asking."

"I'll take Miss Andy back to her mother," Laing said, picking up the little girl, despite her grumbling. "She's getting troublesome."

"No..." Kit started to say, because Laing's departure would leave her alone with Mr. MacNab. And while a reckless part of her might consider that the definition of bliss, native caution warned her to avoid him.

Mr. MacNab was surveying the handcart, with its poor array of holly and pine. "You go ahead, Laing. Kit and I will fill the cart and follow once we're done."

Laing bowed his head. "Aye, sir. There are usually better pickings down in the next glen."

Kit tried to find some assurance in the fact that her stalwart protector saw no danger in sending her off with Quentin MacNab. But then Laing hadn't caught Mr. MacNab's arrested expression when he brushed the snow off her yesterday.

A fuss now would only draw undue attention. So she tugged down the ugly woolen hat she wore as part of her disguise and ducked her head. With reluctant steps, she followed Mr. MacNab deeper into the trees, praying that they came across the world's biggest holly bush within the next few yards. If they filled the cart, they could turn for home and she could disappear into the stables safely away from him.

She told herself that she let her nerves get the better of her. He hadn't said a word to indicate that he thought her anything but a servant and so far, her disguise had fooled everyone at Glen Lyon. She was just edgy around Mr. MacNab because she'd developed a foolish *tendre* for him. When he looked at her, he'd only see a skinny lad.

He took the cart's handle and pulled it behind him across the snow. Because Kit was in a fret, they'd gone a quarter of a mile before she recognized how inappropriate it was for the laird's nephew to do the heavy work.

"Let me take the cart, sir." She added a rough edge to her voice in an attempt to sound more masculine.

"No, I'm fine." He walked well ahead of her. Those long horseman's legs ate up the yards in a way that she couldn't match. "You must be suffering after yesterday."

"A few bruises, that's all. I'm well capable of hauling a half-empty cart."

"Still, better not."

She wanted to argue, but a stable lad didn't defy the laird's nephew.

When Mr. MacNab next spoke, they were descending a snowy path to the next glen. "How long have you been at Glen Lyon now, Kit?"

It was an innocent enough question, but every hair on her skin bristled in alarm. "A month, sir."

"And do you enjoy your work?"

"Aye, sir."

It was true. Most of her life, she'd been lonely, so the company of the other servants here had proven a welcome surprise. She liked the laird and his lady, too. They treated the people who worked for them with a consideration and respect that she appreciated. Glen Lyon had a happy, busy atmosphere that she loved.

"It must be nice to be with your uncle."

"Aye, sir," she said, turning to saw a ragged branch of holly from an unpromising bush. It was a hint that she didn't want to make conversation. A hint Mr. MacNab ignored, to her chagrin.

He stopped a few feet away, and her shoulders twitched under the disreputable coat as she felt him studying her. "Where did you live before this?"

Unfortunately, "Aye, sir," wouldn't cover this one. "Near Inverness," she said shortly, tossing the branch into the cart.

The surrounding quietness suddenly struck her as ominous. She'd imagined that other members of the party would have spread out into this glen, but she and Mr. MacNab seemed to be alone.

"Where, exactly? I know that part of the world quite well."

She bit back an irritated sigh. He would, wouldn't he? "It was a wee, wee village. I doubt you'd ken the place."

"Try me." He'd stepped away from the cart and watched her with a steady concentration that she was sure no humble stableboy merited.

Cold fear oozed down her backbone, and she glanced around the snowy woods in desperation, too flustered to think of making up a convincing lie.

She shivered, then shivered again. The air had turned freezing. Her jumpiness wasn't the only thing making her blood run cold.

"I think we should head back, sir," she said with a hint of urgency. "It's going to snow."

He didn't shift. Nor did he give up on questioning her, devil take him. "Do you miss your parents?"

"I'm an orphan." That at least was no lie. Although she did in fact come from an estate near Inverness further east. She now wished that she'd lied about that.

"I'm sorry to hear that."

"Aye, sir."

She knew he was waiting for her to elaborate on what had happened to her family. But she remained stubbornly silent.

After a while, he heaved a sigh and cast her a wry look. "You're not the world's most talkative soul, are you, Kit?"

"No, sir," she said and hoped he didn't hear the satisfaction in her voice.

"Yet when you're with Andy and William, you chatter away like a magpie."

Heaven help her, this was getting worse and worse. His curiosity about her clearly hadn't started this afternoon. Or even yesterday. He'd been observing her for a while.

So far, her disguise had got her through. Laing kept her away from the other staff as much as he could, and she'd acted the part of a shy, monosyllabic adolescent in the servants' hall with great success. But she had no illusions that if anyone with sharp eyes checked too closely, they would soon dismantle the myth of Kit Laing, self-effacing stableboy. And Quentin MacNab had eyes both sharp and clever, curse him.

"They're good bairns," she said now.

Actually Mr. MacNab was right. Out of everyone on the whole estate, the children were the only people she could relax with. Now she questioned the wisdom of her behavior.

"When they feel like it," Quentin said dryly.

"There's nothing wrong with a bit of spirit, sir." She added the "sir" as an afterthought.

"No, there's not." He continued to study her as if he guessed all her secrets.

Fear made her feel queasy, even as she told herself to bluff it out. There was no reason for Mr. MacNab to take enough interest in her to expose her true identity.

"How long ago did your parents pass away?"

She shifted under that unwavering stare that seemed to see far too much. "My mother died when I was a bairn. My father died two years ago."

Also all true.

"I'm surprised you didn't come to your uncle then."

"My father had married again. I stayed with my stepmother."

"Do you miss her?"

For tact's sake, that question was better left unanswered. "She died, too. Last January."

"I'm sorry to hear that."

"Thank ye, sir."

"So you were cast on local charity?"

"No, sir, I have a stepbrother."

"And is he still alive?"

"Aye, sir," she said tight-lipped.

"You seem to have had a lot of bad luck with relatives dying around you."

"That's nae reason to mock me, Mr. MacNab," she said sharply, before she recalled that a mere stableboy would never rebuke the laird's nephew for his lack of manners. All her instincts screamed at her to run, but something in that steady gaze kept her pinned to the snowy ground, shifting from foot to foot.

"Perhaps not." He kept staring at her.

She'd had foolish dreams of one day appearing before Quentin MacNab as Christabel Urquhart and dazzling him with her charm and beauty. In dreams, she always chose to be charming and beautiful. Why not? But now that she'd attracted his notice, she wished him to Hades.

She needed to get away from him. And she needed to do it now.

"It really is going to snow, sir, and we've wandered a long way from the house." As if to confirm that, a few soft flakes brushed her nose and settled on her eyelashes.

At last he glanced about the woods. His expression told her that until now, he'd paid no heed to her warnings about the weather. "By Jove, you're right. Why on earth didn't you say something?"

She bit back a retort, then noticed the creases of amusement around his eyes. He was teasing her. Which, heaven help her, made him handsomer than ever. He was going to be a favorite with the ladies at the Christmas ball.

Through the worsening weather, they turned back the way they'd come, and Mr. MacNab took the handle of the cart, despite her attempt to retain it. Thickening snow tumbled down around them, turning the woods into a confusing white wilderness. The weather here on the west coast of Scotland could change on a sixpence.

At least the need to get back to Lyon House saved Kit from more questions, but as conditions soon became impossible, she couldn't find too much satisfaction in the reprieve. Vision soon shortened to a few yards, then a few feet, and the temperature dropped with every minute that passed.

Kit stumbled to her knees as she rushed to keep up with Mr. MacNab. "Please lend me your hand, sir," she panted.

He turned and set her back on her feet with capable hands. Despite their danger, a ripple of sensation ran through her at his touch. "This is hopeless. We'll never make it back to the house."

She stared up at him in dismay, as more snow settled on his hair and shoulders. "But what can we do? We have to find shelter."

"There used to be a woodcutter's cottage just off the path here. Let's leave the cart and see if we can find it."

"We can't see anything."

"I've got a pretty good sense of direction. Will you trust me?"

"Aye, sir," she said, to her surprise, meaning it.

"Take my hand and don't let go."

She curled her fingers around his. Despite the danger and two layers of leather gloves, she felt a jolt of heat at the contact. A jolt of heat and a surge of confidence.

Because she'd been watching Quentin MacNab just as closely as apparently he'd been watching her. One thing she'd noticed was that this was a young man remarkable for his competence. If anyone could get them out of this fix, he could.

Common sense told Kit that they only struggled through the snowstorm for half an hour or so, but the time stretched for what felt like forever. The wind had come up, whipping around her and making her shiver. There was no point trying to talk, even if she had the breath for it.

Mr. MacNab never released her hand. That firm clasp made her believe that they were going to make it through this icy wilderness.

Kit should be terrified out of her mind, but even as she sank up to her knees in snowdrifts and breathed air so cold it hurt her lungs, her stubborn heart told her that Mr. MacNab wouldn't let her die.

"Oof!" She crashed into something and gave up what little breath she had.

The something was Mr. MacNab's back. She fumbled to hold onto his thick coat and find her balance. He was shouting something, but even so close, the wind stole his words away. She followed as they stumbled forward, and it took a real effort not to cling to him like a frightened kitten.

She was half-blind with the snow and exhaustion, but soon even she couldn't miss the dark shape that loomed out of the featureless whiteness.

Mr. MacNab released her hand to tug at the door. The small porch provided a bit of shelter, or else she feared the driving snow would have blocked the entrance.

"Damn it, open!" he muttered, and Kit was close enough to hear him this time. He must have been trying to tell her they'd reached the cottage when she ran into him.

She thought she'd been trudging through the snow for a month. It seemed to take another year before the rough wooden door creaked open. The cottage's bulk offered slight protection from the wind, but now she'd stopped moving, she became aware of just how cold it was. If they couldn't get inside quickly, they were in real danger of dying.

"We're in," he said, but his words didn't make sense to her.

"What..."

"Kit, hold on."

She felt giddy as he swung her into his arms and carried her inside, into what seemed like a dark cave. The wind remained loud in here, but compared to outside, the quiet was shocking.

Kit couldn't see a thing. After the struggle through the snowstorm, her sight needed time to adjust to the dimness. Through her frozen stupor, it took her a moment to realize that Mr. MacNab shouldn't be holding her like this. His arms were sure and strong, even after their ordeal outside, but she was a stableboy and he was the master's nephew.

"Put me down," she forced through chattering teeth.

He must have better night vision than she did, because he set her unerringly on a wooden trestle bed in the corner. Although her limbs felt like wet string and her brain was sluggish, she struggled to sit up. It was cold inside the hut, but nowhere near as cold as it was outside.

She felt too vulnerable lying flat on her back. Because of course, she wasn't a stableboy, but a girl in male clothing. While her mind made sense of little else, it recognized that she was alone and unprotected in a virile young man's company.

Don't be a goose, she told herself sharply. He thinks you're a boy. Anyway, nothing you've seen indicates that he's likely to hurt you.

"Ah, that's what I thought. It's still here."

"What...what's still there?" Cold and tiredness for once meant Kit didn't have to add artificial depth to her voice.

"A tinderbox and fuel for a fire. It's been set already. Hamish and Emily must use this place as a shelter. Once I get the fire going, I'll shut the door. At least the hut is sound. I remember it from playing on the estate when I was a boy. Most years, the family came to Glen Lyon for summer holidays."

"You...have a good memory. And a good sense of direction."

Thank God he did. She mightn't want to be alone with Mr. MacNab inside this hut, but it was better than dying out in the blizzard.

"I like to keep my eyes open to what's going on around me."

She stiffened, although surely that wasn't a threat. He couldn't have guessed her secret. Nobody else had. But the reassurances felt hollow.

There were a few scrapes and a crackle, followed by a faint golden glow. Enough light for Kit to make out Mr. MacNab's outline crouched over the hearth.

Compared to the laird, who was a blond giant, Mr. MacNab was much more man-sized. But in this confined space, he appeared dauntingly large. Kit wrapped her arms around herself – for warmth and to quiet her misgivings about how this crisis was going to play out.

"There. That's done it," he said with satisfaction, as the flames caught the kindling. He rose with the athletic grace that she'd noticed from the first and crossed to shut the door.

Immediate calm descended like an axe, although it only seemed calm in comparison to the cacophony outside. "Come close to the fire and thaw out."

"Aye, sir," she said, but when she stood, her legs threatened to fold under her.

Before she landed on the ground in a humiliating huddle, Mr. MacNab was at her side and catching her elbow. "I'm so sorry, Kit. I should have seen the weather was worsening and taken you back to the house. You did warn me. This is all my fault. I wanted to get you alone so I could talk to you."

Her earlier fear rose up to devour her. "I think you should let me go, sir. I can walk."

He ignored her protest and as he helped her to totter toward the fire, she was almost grateful. After he settled her on a three-legged stool, he dragged another one over for himself.

The hut was simply furnished. The bed with its straw mattress. A couple of stools. A rickety table against one wall.

Mr. MacNab removed his wet greatcoat and hung it off a hook beside the mantelpiece. Beneath it, he wore an elegant dark green coat and serviceable black breeches. He sank onto his stool with a weary groan and cast her a concerned glance.

"Here." He held out a silver flask. "It will help."

She accepted it. Despite the crackling fire, she felt frozen right to the bone. "Thank you, sir."

Her hands shook as she raised the flask to her lips. After living with her stepbrother, she was familiar with the scent of whisky.

She took a mouthful and nearly spat it out. How could anyone like this filthy stuff? It tasted like medicine. She swallowed it in a gulp then started to cough. Blinded by tears, she felt Mr. MacNab gently remove the flask from her grip.

She sucked in a breath of air. "That's horrid."

He laughed. "A man develops a liking for it."

Neil certainly had. He always stank of stale spirits. The reminder of what she'd escaped firmed her determination to cling to her disguise. "I can't imagine why he'd want to."

Mr. MacNab laughed. "Is it making you feel better?"

She opened her mouth to say no, then noted the warmth spreading inside her. When she stumbled inside, she'd felt like a block of ice. Now her blood started to flow again. "Aye, sir. Thank you."

"Good." Mr. MacNab lifted the flask to his lips and drank.

She must be feeling better. The foolish girl inside her couldn't help noticing that he drank from where she had. It was as close as she was ever likely to come to receiving a kiss from Quentin MacNab.

Oh, don't be so soppy, Christabel Sophia Urquhart.

"Would you like some more?"

There was a nice little warm space in her stomach that made the awful taste worthwhile, so she surprised herself by saying, "Aye, please."

He smiled with approval and passed over the flask. She took a cautious sip and managed not to choke this time. When she handed it back, she watched him screw the silver cap back on. There was a wicked luxury in being able to study him like this. Everything he did had this marvelous economy of movement that stirred something deep inside her.

Because she was too afraid of people noticing her unsuitable interest in the laird's nephew, she'd only glanced at him in fits and snatches so far. Here in this cottage, she could gaze her full.

Even better, for once, Mr. MacNab wasn't asking any questions. A companionable silence fell, and Kit let her mind drift. It was warm near the peat fire, and the hut kept the dreadful weather at bay. For the first time in weeks, the tight knots of fear in her stomach loosened. When she breathed in, she felt that at last she took in a full measure of air.

"Watch out," a soft, amused voice said, as a strong hand straightened her on the stool. "You're about to slide to the ground."

"Oh, dear, I think it's the whisky." Kit blinked owlishly at him and despite everything, pleasure flooded her.

He offered her such a pleasant view. Those spare intense features with the sharply defined cheekbones. A nose that was just large enough to lend his face character. Eyes full of kindness and intelligence.

He smiled. "I'm now questioning the wisdom of giving you a second dose."

"I'm not used to spirits."

"So I see."

"Do ye think we'll be here for long?" Although even as she spoke, she recognized it as a child's question. How could he know?

"Sometimes storms go for an hour, sometimes they go for days."

Days? Her whisky-induced wellbeing evaporated. How on earth could she keep Mr. MacNab from discovering she was no stableboy, if they were stuck here for days? Even a few hours represented danger. "We cannae stay here that long."

"Let's wait and see." As his eyes rested on her, they were searching. "No point panicking yet."

She couldn't imagine Mr. MacNab panicking in the middle of an earthquake. She, on the other hand, was getting more frightened by the minute. "My...my uncle will be worried."

"I'm sure he will be, but if he and my aunt and uncle have any sense, they'll guess that we found this hut and it's better if we all sit the blizzard out, at least for the moment."

He sounded so sure, she derived a scrap of comfort from his answer. Until she remembered dangers beyond the weather. "We might be here all night."

"We might."

She wrapped her arms around herself. Suddenly she was cold again, despite the fire. "At least we've got plenty of peat."

"We can share the bed, too. Body heat is the best way to keep warm."

No, no, no, no, no. "It's no' fitting, Mr. MacNab." Alarm made her voice shake. "You take the bed, and I'll stay beside the fire."

"Practicality trumps propriety here, Kit."

She frowned in puzzlement. It seemed an odd thing to say to a stableboy. "I'm a mere servant."

"Are you indeed, Kit?" His gleaming hazel eyes fixed on her. "Or should I say rather...Miss Laing?"

CHAPTER THREE

Quentin watched those spectacular eyes widen in horror. The little color Kit had regained since reaching the hut leached out of her face, leaving her as pale as the snow outside.

Her slender throat moved as she swallowed. "I..."

He sliced the air with his hand. "Don't bother denying it. I've had my suspicions for a while, but I knew for sure yesterday when I dug you out of that snowdrift."

Clumsy with terror, she lurched to her feet and dashed for the door, upending the stool in her haste.

Quentin caught her as her frantic hands scrabbled at the latch. He hauled her back against him. "Don't be a wee fool. You won't last ten minutes out there."

"Better that than..."

Nausea cramped his belly. It hadn't occurred to him that she might fear assault, although it bloody well should have. His hold on her wriggling body gentled but not enough that she could escape and run out into the cold.

"Stop it, Kit. You're safe. I swear it on my life."

She kept squirming like a hooked fish. The lass was surprisingly strong, but then he supposed she must be to have played her part as a stableboy all these weeks. It was clear Joseph Laing hadn't singled her out by sparing her any of the hard work. "Devil take you, stand still."

"Will you let me go?"

He hated that she was so scared. Although he imagined fear had been her boon companion for a long time. Only overwhelming fear could have spurred a lass to this desperate masquerade. "I'm sorry I frightened you."

Quentin lifted his hands away and stepped back, hoping that would calm her. Then had to leap forward to grab her around the waist when she headed straight for the door again. "Damn it, Kit. I told you I mean you no harm. Settle down."

This time when he faced her, he kept hold of her arms. He'd learned his lesson.

She was panting, and hatred flashed in her eyes as she glared at him. "You have no right to touch me."

"I do when it's going to save your damn fool neck," he retorted.

His eyes roamed her delicate features. Even in that appalling outfit, she was beautiful. The woolen hat tugged low over her forehead couldn't hide the perfect bone structure or the winged black brows or those flower eyes. That soft, pink mouth never belonged to any stableboy either.

He shook his head in puzzlement. "How the hell did you ever convince anyone that you're a lad?"

That soft pink mouth set in mutinous lines, and she cast him a fulminating look. "I don't have to tell you anything."

"No, you don't." She was like a high-strung filly, flinching at her own shadow and apt to bolt at the merest sound. "But I've kept your secret so far. Won't you trust me?"

She looked bewildered. "You haven't told anyone?"

"No, on my honor." He paused. "And I promise I won't. But you're obviously in trouble. I'd like to help if I can."

"You can help by letting me go," she said sullenly.

"Are you going to take off into the snow?"

She heaved a weighty sigh. "No. You're faster than I am. You'd catch me before I made it."

"Very sensible."

The eyes she raised to his were wary, but the blind panic had receded, thank God. He was poised to chase her again if he had to, but she remained standing in front of him, surveying him as if she expected him to bite her. Quentin wasn't a vain man, but he was used to people liking him, especially the lassies. This fear and suspicion wasn't the usual female reaction to his interest.

As a sign of good faith, he released her arms. "Come back to the fire. It's cold as a penguin's parlor over here."

He turned to right the overturned stool and lowered himself to sit. All the time, he watched the girl, his muscles taut with readiness, in case she made a break for it.

But it seemed she'd accepted his assurances that she was safe, at least for the moment. Hesitantly she picked her way across the floor to collapse in a defeated slump on the other stool.

He pulled out the silver flask and extended it in her direction. "Would you like some more whisky?"

"No, thank you." Whoever she was, she'd been brought up with good manners. But he'd long ago noticed that the new stableboy had a refined air, incongruous in such a low-placed servant. The erratic Highland brogue had disappeared now, too, he noticed.

By God, he needed a drink, even if she didn't. He loathed seeing the dread in her eyes. Whatever she was running from, it was bad enough to have taught her to fear. He hated to think of anyone mistreating this girl, who was such an intriguing mixture of strength and vulnerability. Not to mention so devilish pretty.

He took a mouthful of whisky and slid the flask back into his pocket while he considered the best way of going about gaining her trust. He decided to start with something reasonably simple. "What's your name?"

"Kit."

He bit back a sigh. "No, your real name."

"That is my real name." She bent her head and plucked at a loose thread on that voluminous and hideously ugly coat. Quentin had already worked out that she wore it because she could hide an elephant under there and nobody would know.

He didn't push for an answer and after a moment, she cast him a quick glance from under thick black eyelashes. "You won't betray me?"

He spread his hands to convey his harmlessness. "I haven't yet."

Another silence, while he felt like she weighed his soul in the balance. Then the tense line of her shoulders relaxed a fraction. "My father called me Kit."

"Short for Catriona or Katherine or Christina?"

"Christabel."

"Ah." An unusual name for an unusual girl. Not just because she was dressed as a boy. He'd been watching her since she'd first caught his attention.

Even dressed in the conventional style, she'd be out of the common run of females. "That's pretty."

"Thank you. Mamma loved poetry."

"Coleridge?"

She looked startled. "You know it?"

"I do. It's a strange and beautiful work. The name suits you." He gave a huff of wry laughter. "No, don't go all prickly on me again. I can't help noticing what a bonny girl you are. Nonetheless I can restrain my masculine impulses."

He didn't push for the rest of her name. Not yet.

After a bristling pause, she went on. "To Mamma's dismay, I was more interested in horses than books, so Kit was the name that stuck."

"You're very good with the horses." He kept his voice neutral.

"Horses don't lie, and there's no spite in them."

Something cold hardened her expression, made her look momentarily older. Most stable lads were twelve or thirteen. Quentin had assumed Kit might be sixteen or seventeen, perhaps eighteen. Now he looked more closely, he saw signs of maturity that he'd missed. "How old are you?"

"Twenty, nearly twenty-one."

Not much younger than his twenty-four. "Your parents are still alive?"

If they were, what did they make of their daughter's disappearance? When she spoke of them, he'd heard affection in her voice. Surely they weren't the people who had made her scared enough to embark on this mad escapade. The moment he recognized how afraid she was, he'd discounted the slim chance that she played some prank. Whatever the reasons for her disguise, they stemmed from no idle whim.

Sadness shadowed her large eyes. By God, he'd heard sentimental nonsense about the eyes being windows to the soul, but in Kit's case, it really was true. "Mamma died when I was ten. Papa died two years ago."

Quentin frowned. "So you told me the truth about that?"

"Aye, sir." The answer was a touching reminder of the shy stableboy.

"So the stepbrother exists, too?"

"Aye, sir." The edge to her voice had the hairs prickling on the back of Quentin's neck, and he suddenly felt sick. Had the bastard attacked this beautiful girl, once he had her in his charge?

Her eyes sharpened on Quentin. "No, he didn't assault me."

Quentin sucked in a relieved breath. He abhorred anyone who hurt those smaller and weaker than themselves, but something more powerful than principle revolted at the idea of Kit suffering such horrors. "But he's the man you're hiding from."

It wasn't a question.

"Aye."

"Why?"

She was back to watching him as if she expected him to eat her alive. "I've told you enough."

He had no right to push her. Beyond the right of someone who felt a burning need to protect her. Quite how burning was rather a surprise, although he'd always been a lad with a powerful sense of justice.

Right now, he'd like to take a horsewhip to Kit's stepbrother. Even though Quentin was yet to learn what the bastard had done. It was enough that he'd frightened this gallant girl and placed that haunted look in her eyes.

"Who else knows Kit the stableboy is really Christabel the runaway lady?"

"Mr. Laing, obviously."

Quentin noted that she didn't deny his description of her as a lady.

"He's not your uncle?" But he'd already guessed that.

"No. He was my father's head groom."

More evidence, should he need it, that Kit came from society's upper echelons. Humble crofters didn't have head grooms.

"He's a good man."

"Aye, that he is." For the first time since Quentin had started this interrogation, he caught a hint of a smile on her face. "He put me on my first pony, not long after I could walk. While I was growing up, nobody could keep me out of the stables. Joseph was always kind to me."

"So a natural choice when you needed help?"

She frowned. "I told you I don't want to talk about this anymore."

He rose and threw some more peat on the fire. "You may as well tell me everything, Kit. We could be stuck here for days on end, and we'll need to talk about something."

He was sorry he'd been so flippant, when she lurched to her feet and regarded him in dismay. "Days on end? Surely not."

"Sit down," he said wearily. "I told you you're safe."

She regarded him for an uncertain moment before subsiding back onto the stool. "We don't have anything to eat."

He smiled with what he hoped was reassuring confidence. "Let's worry about that if it turns into a problem. At least there's plenty of peat so we won't freeze."

"If you hadn't found this hut, we could have died out there," she said, her expression somber.

"Don't think about that."

"Lucky you remembered this place."

"I love Glen Lyon and I know it well. The Douglas family is a close one. There are frequent visits in both directions between Hamish and his sisters' families. I'm his sister Prudence's oldest son. My father's estate is in the east near Perth."

"Do you have brothers and sisters?"

As he spoke of his background, Quentin saw her nervousness ease. He supposed it must be a relief to shift the attention away from her plight. Except his attention wasn't away from her plight at all. He hoped if he told her something about himself, she might return the favor.

"Yes, two brothers and three sisters."

"And you love them?"

A smile curved his lips. "They're a blasted nuisance most of the time. Two of my sisters are engaged. One's still in the schoolroom with my brothers."

"I should have known," she said. "You're so good with Andy and Will. It's clear that you're used to dealing with children."

Now that was interesting. It seemed Kit had been watching him, too. "At least I'm used to dealing with my brothers and sisters. I'm fond of the little terrors. I'm sure they'd like you."

She made a strangely wistful gesture. "I would have loved brothers and sisters. You're lucky."

He was. Luckier by far than this jittery girl. "Laing came to Glen Lyon two years ago. That was when your father died."

She went back to looking like she contemplated the end of the world. "Neil, my stepbrother, took over running the estate until I was old enough to take charge. Laing couldn't stomach him as a master, so he found this post at Glen Lyon."

Shock shuddered through Quentin and had him rising to his feet and staring down at the slight woman opposite him. The woman with the unassuming air and the shabby work clothes. The woman who seemed to have convinced everyone except him that she was a humble stableboy.

"By God, I know you who you are."

Fear glittered in her beautiful eyes, as she jerked to her feet once more and backed away. "I told you who I am."

"Aye," Quentin said with an edge. "Kit, also known as Christabel, who has a rare gift with horses and bairns, and a stepbrother who deserves a good thrashing."

"That's right," she said, continuing to watch him warily. And with good reason.

One of Quentin's hands slashed the air. "But you didn't tell me that you're the Earl of Appin's daughter."

CHAPTER FOUR

*Q*uentin saw her attention focus on the door. She tensed up, ready to scarper.

"Don't try it, my lady."

"Don't call me that," she said through stiff lips. He thought she'd been pale before, but now she was almost transparent.

"You're heiress to a fortune."

"Aye."

"One of the greatest in Scotland." He struggled to gather together what he recalled of the Urquhart family and title. It wasn't much. "And you're set up to become countess, because it's one of the few titles that can run through the female line."

"I am the countess," she said, still in that horrid frozen way. She didn't even sound like Kit anymore. Joseph Laing's nephew had always been unusually well-spoken for a servant, but now she sounded like she attended a royal reception. All tight vowels and cut-glass consonants. "I've been the countess since Papa died."

Quentin frowned in bewilderment. "So tell me – what the deuce is the Countess of Appin doing as my uncle's stableboy? I hadn't heard anything about you going missing."

"I suspect Neil is keeping my disappearance quiet to avoid a scandal." She slumped in front of him, suddenly looking exhausted and frightened and defeated. It was as if someone had snipped the strings that held her up. "Please, don't tell anyone."

He resisted the urge to take her arm. She didn't yet trust him enough to let him close. "You have my word."

Startled, she stared into his face. "You mean that?"

"You know I do."

"But you don't know why I've done this hare-brained thing."

His hand swept through the air. "You must have your reasons – and good ones. I can imagine life as Hamish's stableboy is a good deal more arduous than life as the Countess of Appin."

The cynicism that twisted her lips made his heart ache. She was older than he'd originally thought her, but she was too young to look like that. "I've been happy at Glen Lyon."

Which meant she hadn't been happy at Appin. Of course she hadn't been. If she had, she'd never have taken such appalling risks with her reputation and her person.

"I assume Hamish and Emily know who you are."

"Aye."

"Anyone else?"

"I haven't told anyone, but I sometimes think Mrs. McCluskey might have guessed. That I'm a girl, at least."

Mrs. McCluskey, the housekeeper, was one of the cleverest women Quentin knew. She was smart enough to have twigged that the new stableboy wasn't all he appeared to be.

"You can't hope to carry on this masquerade indefinitely," he said. "If I noticed you're not a boy, other people will, too. And as you say, the scandal will be horrendous."

Kit still watched him as though he was a snake about to strike. "It's only until Christmas."

"What happens at Christmas? Do the fairies come down the chimney to save the princess?"

As he'd hoped, that made her smile. He'd noticed that when Kit wasn't scared out of her mind, she liked to laugh. Yesterday during the sledding, she'd been bright and vivid and full of life. Quentin hated to be the person who dulled her light.

"I've spent the last two years wishing the fairies would come and save me. I don't think they exist, even at Christmas."

"Sit down and tell me." He waved toward the stool. "You must know you can trust me."

She didn't move, and the eyes that traveled over him remained old beyond her years. His growing certainty that she was in serious trouble firmed. "Why would I know that, Mr. MacNab? Because you're charming and handsome, and because you're powerfully curious to get me to spill my secrets?"

To his mortification, he blushed. "You've been watching me."

She shrugged. "You're very easy to look at, but as my old nurse used to say, handsome is as handsome does."

"I think you should tell me because I want to help." Self-mockery turned down his lips. "Not to mention, I'm powerfully curious about what would drive one of the richest women in Scotland out of her silken bower and into my uncle's stables."

"I'm not one of the richest women in Scotland. I don't have a penny to my name, unless my stepbrother allows it. And believe me, he never allows it."

Quentin started to develop a healthy dislike for this unknown stepbrother who sounded like a domestic tyrant, at best. At worst, Quentin suspected the bastard had done something heinous to put the fear into Kit's bluebell eyes. He could see this girl had been bullied. How badly, he hoped to find out. But whatever lay behind her terror, he was already on her side.

"So what happens at Christmas?"

She sighed and at last subsided onto the stool. "I become one of the richest women in Scotland."

Something she'd said earlier came into focus. "You turn twenty-one, and you take control of your inheritance."

She nodded. "And Neil Maxwell's rule at Appin will come to an abrupt end." Her tone was flinty, incongruous in such a slight figure, but enough for Quentin to recognize the steel that existed beneath her soft skin.

Of course she was strong. And brave.

Admiration tinged his voice as he returned to the other stool. "Good for you. But couldn't you hold out safely at Appin, if it was only a few weeks until you're free?"

She studied him with a hint of hostility. He didn't appreciate it. Kit might have called him charming and handsome, but he began to suspect that in her book neither word counted as a compliment.

"You're determined to get my story out of me."

"Would it be so bad to confide in me?" He paused. "I've worked most of it out already."

She arched her eyebrows with an aristocratic disdain no stableboy had ever possessed. "Have you indeed?"

He rose and threw some more peat on the fire. The flaring light revealed her face as a combination of beautiful shapes. Again he wondered how anyone had ever believed this girl to be a male.

"Neil Maxwell likes being in charge of your fortune, and he knows you hate him, so he's well aware that his days of access to the Urquhart coffers are limited. The looming danger of Christmas spurred him to do his best to get his hands on the money. He tried to force you to marry him because once he did, he gained permanent control of your fortune."

Quentin prayed that Neil hadn't used violence against the girl. Her skittishness hinted that he had, although she'd said he hadn't. Perhaps the threat of violence had sparked her escape and masquerade.

"Neil didn't want to marry me. The real sticklers wouldn't approve, although it would be legal, I suppose. Neil has political ambitions and doesn't want whispers of a vaguely incestuous marriage to tarnish his chances. Instead, he cooked up a scheme with one of his odious friends. The friend got me and half the money and Neil got the rest." Her dry tone did nothing to hide her loathing for her stepbrother or for his machinations. "I'm sure if Neil could get his hands on everything, he'd try, but he's a gey canny laddie and he knows half of the Urquhart money is better than none."

"Is he young?"

"He's twenty-eight. He's always hated me."

"He's jealous."

"Aye, I suppose so, although he's far from penniless in his own right. He's inherited a substantial property in the Borders. I was twelve when my father married his mother. She didn't like me either."

"You were close to your father?"

A range of emotions crossed her face. Grief and love mainly. "Aye."

"No wonder she didn't like you, especially when you grew up to be a beauty."

She cast him an unimpressed look. "Right now, I doubt if you can tell what I look like when I'm dressed as a girl."

Quentin shot her a straight look. "I can tell."

She surged to her feet, and her gaze fluttered towards the door. How he cursed himself for frightening her again.

He waved at the stool. "Sit down, Kit. I told you you're safe."

The wariness was back. "I have no reason to trust young men."

"Perhaps not, but you can trust me."

When he made no move toward her, she sucked in a shaky breath and sat down again. "I look too much like my mother for Lady Maxwell's convenience. My father loved my mother. He didn't love my stepmother, but he needed a lady for his domains and he hoped that she might be a mother to me."

"I'm sorry. You must have been so unhappy, and missing your mother besides."

"Aye. It wasn't too bad while Papa was alive. He and I always got along well, and Neil was away at school and university for a lot of the time. I escaped to the stables when I could."

It sounded like a lonely childhood, but Quentin forbore from saying so. He gained the impression that Christabel Urquhart, Countess of Appin, was a proud wee thing. She'd loathe knowing that anyone pitied her.

Although his feelings were much more complex than mere pity. He took his hat off to her courage and daring. He feared for her. He hated to think anyone had hurt her.

Not to mention he was a man. She mightn't like him to notice her myriad attractions. But how could he help it?

"The stables where Joseph Laing was head groom."

"Aye. When...when things became impossible and I needed to run away, he was the only one I could turn to."

"Did you have no family to help you?"

"My stepbrother is my legal guardian. If I left Appin as Christabel, he had the right to bring me back under his control. I needed to find a new identity."

"So Kit the stableboy was born."

"Aye. I didn't want Laing to tell the laird and his lady here, but he said he had to."

"Hamish and Emily wouldn't send you back, once they heard your story."

"No, they've been very kind. It was their idea for me to devote most of my time to the bairns."

To keep Kit away from too many inquisitive eyes, Quentin suspected. The less time the new stableboy spent with the other servants, the safer she'd be.

"So tell me about Neil's friend. I'm surprised he didn't try and woo you. It would be easier gaining your consent to a marriage than trying to compel you into one, surely."

A strange, frozen expression entered Kit's eyes and renewed nausea stirred in Quentin's belly. "Kit, are you all right?"

She shook her head as if she banished evil memories. Or at least attempted to. "He did try. As you say, easier all round if I lined up for my punishment without kicking up a fuss." Her voice turned hard. "He was also handsome and charming. At least he was when he wanted something and he thought his winsome ways might get it for him."

Quentin hid a wince at her description. And an unwelcome prick of jealousy. "I'm not like him."

"No, you're not." She leveled an assessing gaze on him. "I knew when I saw how he treated his horses that he was a man with no kindness. He had a ready smile, yet any mount he rode was terrified of him. Horses, dogs and children feel safe with you."

"Thank you." He couldn't help smiling, although nothing about her story pleased him. "I hope you feel safe with me, too."

She didn't smile back. "I don't feel safe anywhere," she said in a bleak tone that made his gut clench with painful compassion.

"So how did the wooing proceed?"

"He moved into the castle, and Neil made sure that his friend and I were alone more than propriety allows. He proposed a week after I met him."

"And you said no."

"Even if I liked him – and I didn't – the last man I'd ever marry was someone hand in glove with Neil."

"I can imagine."

"He proposed a week after that and a week after that. I think by the third time, he and Neil realized that the carrot wasn't working and it was time for the stick."

Horror flooded him and bile was sour on his tongue as he imagined what that meant. "They didn't beat you, damn their greedy hides?"

When she shook her head, relief made him sag on the stool. "They might have eventually, but I was the countess. The clan would have objected. Neil tried locking me in my room and starving me."

"The bastard."

"When that didn't work, his friend threatened to force me. That was when I knew I had to get out."

Quentin desperately wanted to put his arms around her and offer comfort, but he knew she'd view any physical overtures as a threat. How he wished Neil Maxwell and his *handsome, charming* friend were in the room now, so he could beat the two mercenary cowards to a pulp. He was angry enough to take them both on and win.

"Did you climb out the window?"

A faint smile lightened her eyes. "I didn't have to. The castle is full of hidden chambers and passages that I knew about and Neil didn't. I got out of my room one night, made it to the stables, and rode my horse away in search of Glen Lyon, where I knew Laing would help me."

Despite everything, Quentin gave a shout of appreciative laughter. "Good for you." Although he couldn't help shuddering at the thought of the dangers a lone girl faced, riding unprotected across the Highlands. "That's how you survived Neil trying to starve you into submission, too."

"Aye. Neil always thinks he's cleverer than everyone else. It makes him easy to outwit."

"I'm in awe. You must have been absolutely terrified."

The brief amusement faded. "I decided the open road offered no more dangers than I faced at home."

Actually he was complimenting her on everything she'd done. She was a remarkable girl, and one of the most remarkable things about her was that the whole awful narration hadn't contained any hint of self-pity. If there was one thing Quentin admired, it was courage. Christabel Urquhart was the bravest person he knew, male or female.

"So what happens now?"

"I just have to stay hidden until midnight on Christmas Eve, when I turn twenty-one. Then I'll throw Neil and his cronies out of Appin."

"He mightn't go willingly."

"I doubt if he will, but Hamish and Emily have promised to help. Right now, the law is on Neil's side. In a few days, the law will be on mine."

"So Kit disappears and Christabel comes into her inheritance?"

"That's the idea. As long as Neil doesn't find me first." The frozen look returned to her face as she contemplated that possibility.

"Even if he finds you, Hamish and Emily won't hand you over. Anyway, I'll kill the bastard before I let him or his filthy accomplice get their hands on you."

Startled, she looked at him. "Why on earth would you? I'm nothing to you."

That wasn't quite true either. Determination flattened his mouth. "Nonetheless I pledge myself to your cause, my lady."

This time she didn't object to his use of the title. A shy smile softened that lush mouth, and for the first time, she regarded him without any fear. "Thank you."

CHAPTER FIVE

"$\mathcal{I}$s it still snowing?" Kit struggled to keep awake and upright upon her stool.

Already she'd caught herself slipping down toward the dirt floor a couple of times. She'd been up before dawn, mucking out the stables. Laing had made it clear when she asked for his help, that if she wanted to preserve her false identity, she couldn't expect to be treated like the Countess of Appin in the Douglas household. She didn't mind. She liked hard work, and the chance to spend all day with the laird's fine horses was a blessing. But now the fire's warmth and the silence that had descended between her and Mr. MacNab after that long, difficult conversation made her drowsy.

She supposed her torpor must mean she trusted Mr. MacNab, which was unexpected. For so long, she'd been jumping at her own shadow, and she'd been wary of him from the first. In part because he was a handsome young man, and her experiences of handsome young men hadn't been reassuring. In part because everything female in her wanted so badly to trust the laird's magnetic nephew.

It seemed her instincts had been right about Mr. MacNab. As he'd promised when they entered the hut, he made no attempt to touch her or bully her. Which didn't mean she missed the tact and skill he'd employed to coax her story out of her.

How could she resent that, when he placed himself so firmly on her side? He proclaimed himself her champion. When she heard him say that, her heart had risen with sudden hope that she might make it out of this tangle in the end.

Mr. MacNab rose and crossed to the door. The wind was still roaring around the hut. When he managed to heave the door open, the sudden blast of cold made Kit wrap her arms around herself.

The door only stayed open a few seconds before Mr. MacNab battled to close it again. "It's a white hell out there."

"Everyone will be afraid for us."

"There's nothing we can do about it." As he came back to the fire to pile on some more peat, he looked troubled. "It's getting colder, too."

It was. "Do you think we'll be here all night?"

Another nonsensical question, but she found that deep voice so soothing, she didn't really care whether he was speaking calming platitudes.

He rested one elbow on the rustic mantel and cast her a searching glance. "I hope not."

In an odd way, she felt safer here in this primitive hut than she had since she'd run away. If Neil was looking for her, and she had no doubt he was, the dreadful weather would keep him away. She wasn't even afraid of an unmasking anymore, because Mr. MacNab now knew all her secrets — apart perhaps from the foolish penchant she harbored for him.

"Do you trust me, Kit?"

Startled, she looked up, wondering if he'd read her mind. "Aye."

"Thank you." A smile creased his face. "I know you don't trust easily."

"No." She had once, but life had taught her that evil could lurk under an amiable manner, and greed and cruelty didn't always come announced.

"Will you trust me to keep you alive through this snowstorm?"

"Do you want to try and get back to Lyon House?"

His short laugh was dismissive. "Good God, no. We wouldn't make two yards out there."

"Then what?"

"I want to pull the bed near the fire and I want you and I to share it, purely for body warmth. You have my word as a gentleman and a MacNab that I won't take liberties." He paused as if waiting for her to protest. When she didn't speak, he went on. "It's the only way we'll survive this."

Kit waited for her instincts to scream a denial. After all, Belmont Sinclair, Neil's slimy friend, had schemed to winkle his way into her bed. But it seemed she really did trust Quentin MacNab not to try to seduce her and make a claim on her inheritance.

The embarrassing truth was that some wicked part of her might even like it if he did. In the narrow room in the stables, where for a few hours each day she became Christabel instead of Kit, she'd spent too many nights dreaming of his kisses.

"I think that's very sensible," she said calmly and saw his relief at her cooperation. Despite their predicament, a smile tugged at her lips. "I'll spare you a fit of maidenly hysterics. I don't want to die in this hut either. I want to live to kick Neil Maxwell out of my home and watch him scuttle away like the cockroach he is."

Admiration brightened Mr. MacNab's hazel eyes. While she might warn herself to be careful, it was difficult not to bask in his approval. "It would be a tragedy to miss that by a mere week."

"I agree." She rose on legs that felt ridiculously wobbly at the prospect of lying beside Mr. MacNab. It seemed here she was more Christabel than Kit, too. And for weeks, Christabel had concealed a silly *tendre* for this dashing young man. "Shall I help you with the bed?"

"I can manage."

She released a hiss of impatience. "Just because I'm a girl, it doesn't mean you have to treat me like a porcelain figurine. You didn't when you thought I was a stableboy."

"I never thought you were a stableboy," he said quietly.

"Oh," she said, blushing for no reason she could think of.

He sent her another searching look, and she wondered if her weakness for him was quite as much of a secret as she hoped. "Two sets of hands will definitely help with the bed, so thank you, my lady."

She winced. "Seeing we're about to become much better acquainted, you should go back to calling me Kit."

He smiled. "Then you should call me Quentin."

"Oh, I couldn't. Remember I'm officially a servant until Christmas Eve. What would the other servants say if I was suddenly on such terms with the laird's nephew?"

"Fair point. But nonetheless, Mr. MacNab is a little too formal for present circumstances."

She found herself smiling. "Then Quentin you shall be."

The bed was made of solid pine and took a bit of lifting, but they soon had it positioned in front of the roaring fire. Quentin tossed in some more peat before he fetched his now-dry greatcoat and laid it across the straw mattress. "I'm afraid there might be fleas."

"It's too cold for fleas," Kit said, unable to help noting how fine he looked in his shirtsleeves after he removed his green coat.

He gave a grunt of laughter and pointed to her concealing jacket. "Take that off. If we put it over us and wrap my coats around us, we'll preserve more heat."

She regarded him uncertainly. Although he knew who she was, the thick jacket was the main engine of her disguise. Taking it off in another person's presence seemed dangerous.

He smiled and held out his hand. "Come on, Kit."

What a henwit she was. He already knew she was female. Quickly she shrugged off the shapeless jacket and passed it to him. Then before her nerves got the better of her, she lay down on top of his greatcoat.

He took his place behind her so she was closest to the fire. She was painfully aware of him as a large, masculine presence mere inches away from her. He arranged their coverings and settled against the mattress.

Kit told herself to go to sleep, but it was no good. She was too tense, and it still wasn't warm enough. After a short while, she started to shiver.

"I think...I think we'll have to be in contact," she said through chattering teeth.

"Will you mind?"

"I don't want to freeze to death."

"Very well."

He drew her into his arms and back against his chest. She was stiff and awkward, even as a creeping warmth thawed the chill in her blood. She'd never been held by a man before or shared a bed with one, however innocently. Telling herself she could bear this, she closed her eyes and felt Quentin rearrange their makeshift blankets.

"Kit, if you rest flush against me, it will be better."

"Aye," she muttered, scooting across until her back pressed along his front. Already she was warmer. She snuggled closer and tucked her jacket around them more securely.

"Are you comfortable?"

No. She was too aware of his fresh male scent and how he was so much bigger than she was. "It's warmer."

"Aye." He wrapped his arms around her more tightly, and she felt the heat build. "You know you're safe, don't you?"

"Aye," she said, and the strange truth was that she did, although she hadn't felt safe since her father died. "What about you? Are you comfortable?"

"I'm warm," he said. "Any fleas?"

"Not yet."

"Go to sleep. We'll come through this, I promise."

He couldn't know that. The snow could continue for a week. They could run out of peat. They had no food. But despite all that, his confidence eased her heart.

Her rigidity eased, and she instinctively shaped herself against him. It was surprising how natural she felt, lying in a bed with Quentin MacNab.

"They'll come looking for us if we're missing too long," she said.

"Aye, and this hut will be one of the first places they try. I refuse to die a few days before Christmas. It would spoil everyone's festivities."

She'd been sick with fear for so long. Tonight when Quentin uncovered her masquerade, she'd wanted to run out into the snow. Death had seemed preferable to exposing her identity. So it seemed insane that she laughed at the weak joke. "It would indeed."

He shifted so even more of her seemed to be in contact with his body. Her rump pressed into his stomach, and her head tucked in under his chin. "I like to hear you laugh."

All urge to merriment left her. "I haven't had much to laugh about recently."

"I'm sorry, Kit. I despise what you've been through."

Weariness lowered her barriers, dangerously so. "You sound like you mean that."

"I abhor bullies. But if we can keep you alive until Christmas, your toad of a stepbrother will get his comeuppance."

We? There was something heartening in hearing him use that word. She'd held on through this long nightmare. Her clansfolk hated Neil, and their continuing loyalty to the true countess had always infuriated him. Laing and the Laird of Glen Lyon and his wife had been marvelous, too. But when Quentin MacNab put himself so unconditionally at her service, a constricted corner of her heart creaked open to unexpected hope. Perhaps there was a chance that she might prevail.

But she couldn't altogether abandon her customary caution. "If we survive the snowstorm."

Quentin made a dismissive sound that she felt as much as heard. Kit had never been so aware of another person's physical presence. "Pfft. As if a mere bit of Scottish weather will defeat us."

CHAPTER SIX

he creak of the door woke Kit from the deepest sleep she'd enjoyed in years. She opened heavy eyes and for a moment couldn't understand why she wasn't in her pretty bedroom in Appin Castle, with its blue and yellow Chinese wallpaper and huge windows looking out over the hills.

Instead she seemed to be in a dark room, lit by a dying peat fire in a rough hearth. But as would be the case in Appin, she was deliciously warm. And she felt safe, as she'd once felt in her home. She hadn't felt safe for so long that this jerked her back to reality.

Everything that had happened yesterday returned in a flash. Quentin's unwelcome questions. The snowstorm. The long, difficult conversation in front of the peat fire. Sleeping in Quentin's arms.

Those arms tightened around her now as the door opened and what seemed like a crowd of people rushed into the hut. The sky outside was clear and the pale blue of early morning.

"Praise the Lord you're here and safe," Mr. Douglas said in his deep rumble of a voice. His heartfelt gratitude at finding the two of them alive made Kit's ears vibrate. "We feared you were lost."

Quentin shifted behind her and rolled out of the bed to stand. Kit, agonizingly conscious of the danger of discovery, struggled back into her concealing jacket. She was so clumsy with sleep that it took her longer than it should.

"We were lucky the hut was nearby when the blizzard started." Quentin moved around the bed and used his body to offer her a modicum of cover.

She appreciated his quick thinking. In fact, as she recalled the night just passed, she appreciated everything he'd done. True to his word, he'd made no advances. Only now when rescue arrived did she suffer a moment of sinful regret over that.

"Nephew, are ye unharmed?" Laing asked, frowning down at her with a concern that reminded her yet again of how kind he'd always been to her.

Kit looked up blearily and the crowd of people dissolved into the laird, Laing, and three of the grooms. She mustered a shaky smile, feeling more secure now she was concealed under her jacket's bulk. "Aye, Uncle. But I'm gey hungry."

She wasn't trying to be funny, but her answer had them all laughing. She heard sheer relief in the humor, and she started to laugh herself.

Quentin extended his hand to help her to stand. Just like that, she was afraid.

A gentleman might assist the Countess of Appin to her feet, but he'd never offer a hand to a scruffy stableboy. She shook her head at him and saw him realize what he was doing. Instead, he grabbed his crumpled greatcoat and flung it around his shoulders.

"We'll get you back to Lyon House for a good breakfast, lad," Hamish said.

"Is it still snowing?" Quentin asked.

"No, it stopped before sunrise. We came out after you as soon as we could. If it was possible, we would have come yesterday."

"You'd have risked your lives if you had," Quentin said. "We were safe here."

"Aye, you were," Hamish said. "We hoped you might have found the hut. You spent so much time running over the estate when you were a lad, I thought you'd remember it."

One of the grooms brought in a bucket of snow to douse the fire. The other two lifted the heavy bed back against the wall. Soon the hut would reveal no trace of Kit and Quentin's occupancy.

Yet momentous things had happened here, things she needed to come to terms with.

"We brought the ponies so you'll get a ride back home," Laing said.

Nausea cramped Kit's belly, as she realized that the real reason that they'd brought the horses was because they weren't sure whether they'd find bodies. Scottish weather could kill. Without Quentin's knowledge of the glen and his resourcefulness, she'd be lying frozen and stiff in some snowdrift.

She glanced up to meet somber hazel eyes and realized that he, too, recognized the real danger they'd been in last night. Hamish and Laing were talking about earlier snowstorms and the grooms had gone outside, so she risked a whispered thank you. He dipped his ruffled head in an imperceptible bow.

When the summons arrived to attend Lady Glen Lyon in her parlor, Kit was cleaning tack in the stables. It was late afternoon of the day that she and Quentin had been rescued from the hut. In view of her trials, she'd been given some time off, but after a huge breakfast and a couple of hours' sleep, she'd woken wanting to do something useful.

Cleaning tack was one of those endless jobs that never seemed to be done and most of the grooms hated it. But Kit rather liked sitting alone in a warm room, breathing in the rich, leathery smell of the saddle soap. She certainly loved watching the harness turn all gleaming and buttery soft. And one thing was for certain – none of her colleagues were likely to volunteer to help her, so she was safe from discovery for a little while.

When Emily's maid Polly found her, the girl was flustered and annoyed. "I've been all around the houses looking for you." Polly had come up to Glen Lyon from London after the laird's marriage, but all these years in Scotland and four years of marriage to the head gamekeeper had done nothing to soften the Cockney in her voice.

Kit put down the bridle she worked into suppleness. "Well, I didn't know, did I? What is it?"

Polly sent her a displeased look, fitting from a lady's maid to a lowly stableboy. "None of your sauce now, young Kit. Her ladyship wants to see you quick smart, so tidy yourself up and get over to the house."

Panic tightened every muscle in Kit's body, and her heart began to race. Since her first day here, when Laing had presented her to Emily and Hamish as the runaway Countess of Appin, she hadn't been inside the family's apartments. This order to attend the laird's lady struck her as alarming in the extreme.

"What does her ladyship want?" Kit asked nervously, standing and shoving her hands in her pockets so Polly wouldn't see how they shook.

Polly frowned. "She didn't say." Which was clearly also a source of displeasure. "And it's not for you to ask. So have a wash and get over there. I've already been looking for you for half an hour."

Had her stepbrother come? Was the game up?

Stuck in the back room of the rambling stable complex, Kit wouldn't hear if someone arrived. When Polly left, she wondered if she should steal a pony and take off for the hills. At the very least, she could hide in the hut where she'd slept last night.

She made herself suck in a deep breath to steady her swimming head and told herself to settle down. She'd learned to save her trust for the few people who deserved it. So far she trusted Laing. And Hamish and Emily had done their best all these weeks to keep her secret and provide a haven. And last night, she'd trusted Quentin.

If Neil turned up, she couldn't imagine that the Douglases would merely hand her back to him without a qualm. They'd be more likely to hide her somewhere secure. After all, it was only a few days until Christmas and her freedom from her stepbrother's tyranny.

Still, she was almost sick with apprehension when she climbed the steps to the laird's opulent apartments. No visitors had arrived at Glen Lyon House, but perhaps Neil had written. A communication from Appin could be the only reason Emily would call her in.

When she entered the high, airy room with its view over the beautiful sea loch and the ring of surrounding hills, now cloaked in white, only Emily and Quentin waited for her. That did little to soothe Kit's fears, and once the footman who had shown her the way had gone, she stepped forward.

"Is it Neil? Has he found me?"

Emily cast a curious glance at Quentin. "I'm to assume that the Countess has told you her secret?"

Kit turned to Quentin, startled. "You didn't tell Emily you know who I am."

He shook his head. At her arrival, he'd stood as a gentleman should for a lady. She had a sick feeling that his good manners were more likely to arouse suspicions about her identity in the people of Glen Lyon than anything he said.

"I've only just arrived." He resumed his place in the carved oak chair beside the blazing fire. "Anyway I swore I wouldn't tell anyone."

Emily sat on the window seat. She indicated for Kit to sit next to her. "That's a relief. This makes it easier to say what I need to."

Kit stayed where she was, dread pounding in her veins. "Has Neil written?"

"No. You're still safe." The reassurance in Emily's smile went some way toward easing Kit's agitation. "I'm sorry if I gave you a fright."

A flood of relief made Kit's knees loosen like wet string. As she crossed to sit beside Emily, she released the breath she felt like she'd been holding since Polly had found her. "I nearly took off."

"It's a good thing you didn't." Emily directed a disapproving frown at her. "We've already had quite enough search parties out after you."

"It was my fault that we were caught in the blizzard," Quentin said. "I had my doubts about the new stableboy's identity, and I wanted to get him – her – alone so I could ask some questions."

"Kit's disguise didn't fool you?" Emily settled shrewd eyes on him and to Kit's surprise, debonair, self-confident Quentin MacNab blushed to his ears.

"I was never convinced that she was a boy. I knew for a fact she wasn't, once I dug her out of the snow after the sled turned over."

"I feared the disguise might not deceive anyone who looked too closely," Emily said soberly. "I'm surprised it's succeeded as long as it has."

"To me, she's always looked like a pretty girl pretending to be a boy. I must have seen this particular plot a hundred times in the theater."

"Perhaps people up here haven't been to the theater as often as you have," Kit said.

Emily gave an appreciative huff of laughter. "I'm sure that's true, but that doesn't change the fact that if Quentin has noticed you're a female, someone else might."

"Quentin is cleverer than most people," Kit said, earning a smile from him and a thoughtful stare from Emily.

"Nonetheless, I'd rather the world didn't know that Scotland's richest heiress is grooming my horses from dawn to dusk every day."

Kit had been nervous since the summons had arrived. Now genuine fear iced her blood, as she rose on unsteady legs. "Are you...are you sending me away?"

Beneath her fear lurked other unpleasant emotions. She'd found a home at Glen Lyon, a home she'd lost at Appin when her father remarried. She might be engaged in humble work, but she enjoyed it. She liked being useful.

More than Glen Lyon the place, though, she'd miss the people. Stoic, taciturn Laing. The other grooms. The laird's lively children. Emily and Hamish. The cheerful household staff.

The prospect of leaving Quentin MacNab cut deepest of all. Although Kit knew she risked betraying her penchant for him, her gaze settled on him. She'd never spoken to anyone as honestly as she had to him last night. She'd never felt anyone understood her so well. And sleeping in his arms had been a pleasure she'd love to experience again.

Of course, that could never be. The Countess of Appin was prey to all the strictures of society, strictures that didn't apply to Kit the stableboy.

Even now, Quentin leaped to her defense. And to his feet. "Emily, you can't throw the girl to the wolves. You know what her stepbrother will do if he gets his hands on her. If you don't want to offer her shelter any longer, I'll take her to Mother. Kit will be safe at Cannich House and by the time Neil thinks to look for her there, she'll be of age and free of his filthy clutches."

A private joke seemed to amuse Emily as she surveyed Kit and Quentin. "I feel like I'm back in the theater, and the hero has just marched onstage to vanquish the villains. Sit down, both of you. I have no intention of sending Kit away. Hamish and I offered her ladyship our help when she arrived and that hasn't changed. Especially as it's only a few days until she comes into her majority."

Something in Emily's calm certainty blunted the edge of Kit's panic. She drew a shaky breath and told herself to stop being so jumpy.

"Thank you, Emily." She sent Quentin a grateful smile. Emily might mock his immediate defense of her, but Kit hadn't had enough champions in her life to scorn his gallantry. "And thank you, Quentin. You're too good."

To her delight, he turned pink again. "Not at all."

Her heartbeat slowing, Kit subsided onto the window seat. "So what are you suggesting, Emily?"

The humor drained from Emily's fine eyes and compassion took its place. "Now don't go flying up into the boughs again. But I believe the time has come to retire Kit the stableboy and introduce Christabel, Lady Appin, to the audience."

"But I remain under Neil's legal control." Kit stiffened, while every atom in her body shouted denial. "What if he learns I'm here?"

Emily's smile remained reassuring. "Have a little faith, Kit. Neither Hamish nor I will hand you over, even if he turns up with every constable in Scotland. I can see that Quentin has declared himself your protector, too. We only need to keep you until Christmas, then you're free. A bunch of Douglases are canny enough to outwit any Maxwell."

Disquiet churned in Kit's stomach. "But everyone on the estate will know that I've been here in disguise. Putting me into a dress won't convince people that they've never seen me before."

"That's true. Hamish and I think we should tell the clan something of your story."

Quentin was frowning. He, like Kit, must be working through the implications of this new plan. "So we enlist the locals in the scheme to keep Kit safe?"

"Yes. They're all loyal to Hamish and if he asks them to help, they will. Not to mention that you've found a place in their hearts, Kit."

"But that was before they knew I lied to them," she said grimly, already disliking the prospect of playing the fine lady again. She might have spent the weeks at Glen Lyon being afraid, but she was used to that. Frightened or not, Kit had been free in a way Christabel could never be.

"They'll understand. They might even like it," Quentin said, leaning one elbow on the mantel and looking thoughtful. "As Emily said, this is like a play or a fairy tale."

"Exactly." Emily caught Kit's trembling hand in hers. "It will all work out, Kit. We brought you this far. We'll get you safely to the end."

Kit summoned a shaky smile. "You've been so kind. And you've taken such risks. You broke the law the moment you offered me your help, and with every day since, you've embroiled yourself deeper in my troubles. How can I ever repay you and Hamish?"

"Pish." Emily might have lived in the Highlands for the last six years, but she still sounded as English as a Melton Mowbray pork pie. "This is the kind of tale we'll tell our grandchildren. How we sheltered a princess in disguise from the ogres bent on her destruction."

Kit gave a snort that would have made people look askance at the Countess of Appin. "A princess who stinks of straw and saddle soap – and worse."

Emily smiled back. "That's the best sort of princess."

"Hear, hear," Quentin said.

Emily's humor faded until she looked deadly serious. "Which brings me to the other reason I asked to speak to both of you."

Foreboding gripped Kit. "What is it?"

Emily's grip on her hand tightened. "Kit the stableboy could spend a night alone in a hut with the laird's nephew with no questions asked. Not so much the Countess of Appin."

Kit ripped her hand away and sprang to her feet once more. "But nothing happened."

Quentin remained by the hearth, but his expression turned troubled. "On my honor, Aunt Emily, we did nothing to be ashamed of."

"I happen to believe you." A faint smile hovered around Emily's lips. "You only call me your aunt in moments of extremity."

His perturbed expression didn't ease. "The countess is as pure as the day she was born."

Emily's stare was uncompromising. "You're talking like a child, Quentin. You know it's appearances that count. Everyone in the glen knows you and Kit were together all night. Kit's going to have to do her best to smother a scandal anyway, once she takes over her inheritance. Having her painted as a scarlet woman will be a step too far."

Kit couldn't help noting through her own horror that Quentin didn't seem too eager to accept the consequences of his actions. It shouldn't hurt, but it did.

"The countess is hiding at Glen Lyon to avoid a marriage she doesn't want. It would be too ironic if she's forced to make one anyway," Quentin said hotly, straightening away from the mantelpiece. "The clan will keep quiet about anything that happened last night."

Emily shook her head with a fond exasperation that did nothing to discount the gravity of their dilemma. "Too many people are privy to the facts. We might restrict the knowledge of Kit's identity to people on Glen Lyon for a few days. No longer. News of Kit's night with you will spread out across the Highlands sooner rather than later, and her reputation will be ruined." Emily glanced between Kit and Quentin. "I'm afraid you two need to get married."

CHAPTER SEVEN

Quentin stared across to where Kit – Christabel – stood straight and still in front of the window. He read the frozen horror on her face.

By heaven, what else could he expect? She'd launched this whole dangerous enterprise to escape an unwelcome husband. Now here she was staring down the barrel of a forced marriage. No wonder she looked as sick as a dog, poor wee lassie.

Although he'd thought she liked him. He squashed an unworthy pang at seeing how little appeal the idea of marrying him held. Especially as for him, the idea of life with Christabel Urquhart was infernally appealing.

"Would...would a betrothal not serve as well as a marriage?" Kit asked in a quavery voice that didn't sound at all like the valiant girl who had been such a stalwart companion through last night's vicissitudes. "At least until after Christmas when we've had a chance to assess how bad any scandal is likely to be."

"I'm afraid not, Kit. A broken engagement after the fact will only fuel gossip." Compassion softened Emily's face. "Being stuck like this isn't the end of the world, even if it might feel like it right now. Quentin knows how my marriage started out, but you probably don't. Hamish and I wed to scotch a scandal, too, and we were as innocent of wrongdoing as you are. In fact, you and Quentin are better off than we were. At least you two seem to get along. Hamish and I had known each other for years and we'd spent most of that time fighting like cat and dog."

Kit's eyes rounded with astonishment. Those lovely blue eyes that betrayed her every emotion. How in Hades anyone had ever believed this exquisite girl was a boy continued to leave Quentin flabbergasted. Not just a boy, but a rough-and-tumble stable lad at that.

"But you're so happy together," Kit said.

Emily's smile widened. "We are, but we spent most of our first year of marriage living apart. I thought marrying Hamish was the greatest mistake I ever made, yet it's turned into a glorious blessing from heaven."

This encouragement didn't seem to reassure Kit, who looked like a fox facing a slavering pack of hounds. "You were lucky."

"We were. But that doesn't mean you won't be, too."

"It doesn't mean we will be either," she said flatly.

Emily sent them another of those searching looks that seemed to see things Quentin couldn't. "You're starting out ahead of us. You like each other."

"Her ladyship is everything that's admirable," Quentin said. "How could anyone fail to like her?"

He saw Kit hide a wince at the use of her title. "And of course I like Quentin."

Quentin hid his own wince at the lack of conviction that statement conveyed.

"If you two wed, there is the added benefit that Kit will be safe from her stepbrother all the sooner," Emily said. "A rushed marriage may present a few legal issues, given Maxwell remains Kit's guardian while she's underage, but so close to Christmas, he'll be in no position to take action against it. Anyway Kit turns twenty-one on Christmas Day, so I imagine the courts will see any case he makes as too little too late."

"You've...you've thought of everything," Kit said, not sounding particularly pleased.

"But it's not up to me, is it?" Her expression determined, Emily rose from the window seat. "You two need to talk this out. I'll leave you now. Come and find me when you've reached a decision. I'll be in the library. There is always so much to do, with Christmas and the ball coming up. If you're going ahead with a wedding, we need to talk to the minister. And we need to start Kit's transformation back into Christabel."

Quentin wanted to object to Emily giving the impression that they had any choice. He was well aware that Emily was leaving him alone with Kit so he could propose.

Still, he appreciated the chance to speak to Kit and chase that stricken expression from her pretty face. "Thank you, Aunt Emily."

Emily sent him an encouraging smile then stopped in front of Kit. "May I hug you?"

The desolate look in the eyes Kit raised to his aunt threatened to break his heart. She wasn't far from crying. She hadn't cried when she fell off the sled or when they'd been lost in the snow. But the prospect of marriage to Quentin MacNab had her looking like she faced the end of the world. A sour mixture of regret and chagrin stewed in his gut.

"I'd like that."

Emily put her arms around Kit's slight form and held her close. "If you say yes to this charming rascal, I'll be very happy to welcome you into the family. Hamish and I like you, and we've admired your spirit from the first."

Quentin's stomach clenched with more pity when he heard Kit muffle a sniff as she pulled back. Her eyes were bright with unshed tears. "You and the laird have been so kind to me. You're still being kind to me."

Emily made a dismissive sound. "Nonsense, child. We're the lucky ones. You've been the world's greatest stableboy."

That drew a husky little chuckle from Kit. The sound made Quentin feel slightly less hopeless. "It was the least I could do."

"You'll do, your ladyship." Emily kissed her on the pale cheek. "I'll be proud to call you my niece."

"I'm out of the habit of hearing myself called her ladyship. Kit, your stableboy, received greater kindness than Christabel Urquhart has over recent years. And more respect. Thank you, Emily. I can never repay you, whatever happens now."

"It will all work out. Just you wait and see." Emily gave her another brief hug and stepped back. "Christmas at Lyon House is always a magical time. Happy endings guaranteed."

Another of those delicious little chuckles, and Quentin was relieved to see that Kit didn't look nearly as forlorn as she had a few moments ago. It made his task easier. He had no intention of bullying her. She'd been bullied enough. But he felt like a bully when he contemplated the best way to convince a frightened, defenseless girl to marry him.

Once Emily had gone, a thorny silence descended. Quentin stepped away from the fireplace but was careful to keep his distance from Kit. She might appear less terrified, but he feared she'd take to her heels if he made any sudden movement. He'd tamed enough wild creatures in his time to recognize her trembling stillness as barely contained panic.

"Shall we talk about this, Kit? Or would you rather think everything through first? I'm completely at your disposal."

A wary gaze leveled on him, but when she spoke, her tone was apologetic. "I'm so sorry I got you into this mess. I'm sure you don't have to marry me."

He was sure he did. He just wished the idea left the bride looking a little less woebegone. "What about your reputation?"

One hand batted the question away. "Once word gets out about me playing a stableboy – and it will – my reputation will be ruined anyway. At best, the world will call me an irredeemable hoyden. Falling prey to the laird's nephew will just seem part of the pattern."

"Don't you care?"

Her shoulders slumped, and he read despair beneath her fear as she dropped onto the window seat in a disconsolate huddle. "Of course I care." Her tone was wooden. "I always imagined I'd lead a conventional life. A season. Presentation at court. Suitors. Falling in love with a good man. Marriage. But none of that has happened. Instead, Neil has used the letter of the law to keep me a prisoner, and escaping him meant I broke every rule in the book. I stopped being an acceptable match for any decent man the moment I cut my hair and rode away from Appin Castle. That girl I was before Papa died no longer exists, just as the life she would have led is no longer possible."

Her sadness sliced a bloody wound across his heart. She didn't deserve any of the awful things that had befallen her, and now it looked like a hasty marriage would top all the other calamities.

"What will you do if we don't wed?"

She shrugged with unconvincing carelessness. "I'm the Countess of Appin. I still control vast property on the east coast. All isn't lost. I'll stay on my estates, I'll race my horses, I'll make sure I lead a full life, if only to cock a snook at my vile stepbrother."

What a gallant girl she was. He admired her bravery more than he could say, but it all sounded rather lonely. "There will be men willing to overlook the smudges on your good name, especially once time passes."

A bleak smile turned down her lips. "I've gone to such lengths to avoid falling into a fortune hunter's hands. I have no intention of leaping from the frying pan into the fire."

"I'm not interested in your fortune," he said, hoping to glory she believed him. He'd be damned if she put him in the same category as Neil Maxwell or his oily swine of a friend. "My estates mightn't compare to yours, but when the time comes, I'll inherit more than enough to keep me in brandy and cigars. In fact, from what I can see, your fortune hasn't done you an ounce of good. Instead, it's caused you a mountain of pain."

The tension eased from her face, and he caught a welcome glimpse of a fledgling animation. "But when I gain control of my money, I can do an awful lot of good with it, assuming Neil hasn't spent me out of house and home. He's hidden the accounts from me for years, but I'm my father's daughter. I can see how he's mismanaged the estate. Once I've rid Appin of this plague of Maxwells, I can start to rebuild. That will keep me busy while the world wastes its time, gossiping about the scandalous countess who ran around the countryside in breeches."

Quentin sighed and folded his arms as he stared down at her where she sat on the window seat. "You're wrong, you know."

She looked startled. "About what?"

"Let's start with doling out responsibility for our predicament. You seem to blame yourself for this tangle, but the mess isn't your fault. It's mine. If I hadn't tried to get you alone so I could satisfy my curiosity, there wouldn't be any talk about us spending the night together."

She cast him a quick glance, and he could see he was far from convincing her. "You meant no spite."

"I didn't, but that doesn't alter the result."

The light flooding through the window behind her revealed the purposeful set of her chin. "You don't want to marry me."

He wouldn't say that, but he could see now wasn't the time to tell her that he found her enchanting. If he confided what he really thought of her, she might even wonder if he was one of those fortune-hunting gentlemen. To Hades with that notion.

So he kept his tone neutral. "Marriage wasn't something I was planning right now, no."

"You see, then? Emily means well, but we can go on without an engagement."

He frowned as he unfolded his arms and dared to take a step toward her. "You've got it all worked out, but you've forgotten one thing, Kit."

The wariness returned to her expression. How he itched to eviscerate Neil Maxwell for stealing all the trust away from this lovely girl. "I told you I don't give a fig for the damage to my reputation."

It was his turn to give her a bleak smile. "That's all very well. But what about the damage to my reputation?"

"Your reputation?" she echoed in bewilderment.

Quentin sat down beside her. He was almost certain that they'd passed the stage where she was likely to take off. "Aye, my reputation. I don't particularly fancy spending the rest of my no doubt blameless life tarred as the man who seduced the innocent Countess of Appin, then refused to restore her honor."

"Oh."

The glum little sound expressed a world of unhappiness. He supposed he couldn't blame Kit for being miserable. She'd struggled so hard to avoid the trap of marriage, but escape was now out of reach. She stared down to where her slender fingers twined together in her lap.

"Oh, indeed."

He let the silence continue. She needed time to work through the implications of their situation.

Finally, she raised dull eyes to his. "I'm so sorry, Quentin. You must be cursing the day you met me."

Despite the fraught atmosphere, he gave a short laugh. "No need for melodrama. I like you, Kit. I think Emily is right. Despite how we're beginning, we might have a chance of making a go of things."

She didn't smile back. "I don't deserve you."

"Enough of that." He felt himself blush. "But I mean you to know that I have no interest in your blasted fortune. If we're going to do this, I want papers drawn up that give you control of all the Appin assets."

Delicate eyebrows arched in surprise. "You'd do that?"

"Without a second thought." He paused. "So you may rest assured that you can go ahead with any plans to restore the estate. In fact, I hope you'll let me help."

"I'm still not sure that you have to do this drastic thing."

"Marry a pretty girl and save her from the wolves baying around her? It doesn't seem that drastic to me."

She didn't smile. "A girl who will be the talk of Scotland, once the tale gets out."

He shrugged. "A lot of people will say it's romantic, like a fairy tale. Emily is right about that, too. If we show the world how virtuous we are at heart, eventually the tattle will turn in our favor."

"You're an optimist," she said with a hint of sourness.

"I am." He dared to reach out and take her hand. He'd held her in his arms all night and never for a moment had he forgotten she was female. But when he took her hand now, it felt in an odd way like the first time he touched her. "I think...I hope I can teach you to be an optimist, too, if you'll let me."

Quentin waited for Kit to pull away, but she contemplated their joined hands with an unreadable expression. She looked much older than twenty. He promised himself that if she took him on, he'd show her that life could still hold joy and goodness.

His grip tightened, and he spoke in a low voice. "My lady, would you do me the inestimable honor of becoming my wife?"

When she didn't answer immediately, his heart sped up. It felt like an hour before she lifted her gaze to his face, although common sense said it could only be a few minutes. Her expression was stern and her eyes were lightless, but her jaw was set with determination.

"Thank you, Mr. MacNab. I accept."

CHAPTER EIGHT

From where Kit stood halfway up the grand sweep of the staircase, she watched the latecomers sidle in to join the restless crowd. The entire staff, inside and outside, of Lyon House had assembled in the hall below her.

It was the morning after she'd accepted Quentin's proposal. Curious eyes fixed on the party gathered on the steps, and she could hear a questioning murmur as the servants noted that Kit the stableboy was now dressed as a girl.

Emily and Hamish stood on the first landing, with Quentin and Kit together a few steps higher. Andy and William waited below with their nurse, wide-eyed and uncharacteristically silent as the portentous atmosphere dampened even their high spirits.

This was uncomfortable. Kit felt like she was on a stage. Which was of course why Emily had arranged it this way.

Kit was sick with nerves and guilt. Nobody liked being exposed as a liar, and she'd lied to almost everyone at Glen Lyon since the day she'd arrived.

Would her former colleagues hate her? Would they betray her to her stepbrother?

She felt some small relief when Laing looked up to give her a brief smile. Without his help, she couldn't have managed this masquerade at all. She owed him so much, and she tried to convey that gratitude in the smile she returned to him.

"Don't be afraid," Quentin murmured at her side.

He'd dressed carefully for this gathering, in a stylish black coat and a white neck cloth, tied in a more elaborate knot than he usually wore. As Kit the stableboy had been achingly aware, Quentin was a good-looking man. Today he was dazzling.

"I'm always afraid," she said flatly.

His gaze was steady. "I hope to change that."

"I don't want them to despise me."

"They won't despise you." A faint smile curled his mouth. "They'll love claiming a part in the grand adventure."

"It doesn't feel like a grand adventure." She heard that weak little response with self-disgust. Sucking in a breath, she squared her shoulders. Her father would be ashamed of her for being so spineless. An Urquhart could do better. "Oh, listen to me feeling sorry for myself. I apologize for making such a poor show."

Quentin's smile didn't falter. "I've never met anyone as brave as you, and a few nerves at a time like this aren't out of place at all."

"What about a full-blown panic?" Although his praise eased her tension.

"Even that." He ran an admiring gaze over her. "You make a bonny girl, by the way. I knew you would."

Kit glanced down at Emily's royal blue merino gown that Polly had made over to fit her. It was in the first stare of fashion, with pretty looping black velvet trim on the hem and cuffs. "After all these weeks in breeches, it feels strange to wear a skirt."

Laughter lit Quentin's eyes to bright gold. "That dress wouldn't be very practical for mucking out the stables."

"No. I suppose not." Self-consciously she touched her hair. "And Polly did her best to change Kit's crop into something feminine."

Polly had worked magic with the scissors. Kit's black hair feathered around her face in a much more flattering style than the rough mop she'd chopped it into before escaping Appin.

"She did a lovely job. You'll set a new fashion. They'll call it the countess crop."

Kit muffled a laugh. He was making her feel better, which didn't seem fair when she was about to ruin his life. "Thank you."

"It looks devilish becoming. Stop worrying."

She sent him a serious glance. "Thank you for bolstering my spirits."

His smile broadened. "That's my job."

As Hamish raised his hand, Emily shot them a meaningful look. The confused hubbub below faded to charged silence. As if guessing that Kit's heart raced with trepidation, Quentin caught her hand. Immediate warmth flooded her, and she clung shamefully tight to his fingers.

"Trust me, Kit," he said under his breath. "I won't let anything bad happen."

Absurd as it was, she believed him. So when she faced the crowd, she stood straight and proud.

"You must all wonder why I brought you in here today," Hamish began, his resonant voice effortlessly filling the large space. "You all know Kit, who has become a valued member of our household over the last weeks. Well, Kit isn't quite what he seems. In fact, Kit isn't Kit at all, but Christabel Urquhart, the Countess of Appin, who has sought refuge with us."

Kit watched astonishment fill so many faces as a buzz of shock assailed her ears. She experienced her own surprise when she noticed that not everybody seemed taken aback by the news. Was it possible that her secret wasn't such a secret after all?

Hamish went on, recounting the tale of oppression and escape with such *élan* that Kit couldn't help feeling that he made her sound like a heroine from a novel. She shifted awkwardly from one slippered foot to another, as acts of sheer desperation became in his account feats of daring bravery.

"It wasn't like that," she murmured to Quentin. "He's turning me into Joan of Arc."

"I'm hoping this story has a happier ending than hers."

She muffled another giggle. Never had she imagined deriving any enjoyment from the exposure of her identity, but she hadn't counted on Quentin's wry sense of humor.

"So, people of Glen Lyon who have adopted Kit as one of your own, I hope you'll be equally ready to protect Lady Appin," Hamish said in a ringing tone, as if he called his clan to battle. "We only need to keep her safe until Christmas Day, when she's free of her stepbrother's control. What say you?"

To Kit's surprise, a resounding cheer rose from the crowd, with shouts of approval for her actions. As Quentin squeezed her hand, she blinked away a rush of tears.

"I told you they'd be on your side," he said softly.

Hamish raised his hands again to quiet the hullabaloo. "I have even happier news to share.

Reverend Kinney is waiting in the library now to join her ladyship and my nephew Quentin MacNab in holy matrimony. Lady Glen Lyon and I couldn't be more delighted that these two exceptional young people have decided to spend their lives together. Tomorrow night's ball will celebrate not just Christmas, but a new family member. Tonight, the celebrations belong to the clan. I invite you all to a ceilidh to mark a wedding in Glen Lyon."

This time the cheering was loud enough to raise the rafters, and Kit found herself smiling at the unbridled enthusiasm.

That smile faded abruptly when Quentin bowed and presented his arm. "The minister awaits, my lady."

Troubled, she stared into those changeable hazel eyes. She searched for some sign of the reluctance she knew he must feel. But all she saw was his innate kindness and something that looked like affection.

What else could she expect? Quentin was too much of a gentleman to betray anything but gracious acceptance of the fate that awaited them.

Kit mustered her faltering courage, as worry and remorse coiled like poisonous snakes in her belly. Because while she could think of nothing she'd like better than a lifetime with this wonderful man, she was well aware that he put a good face on a duty he couldn't avoid. She wanted him with every beat of her heart, but he deserved so much more than this hurried wedding to smother a scandal and save her skin. It broke her heart how hard he fought to hide his real feelings from her.

Right now, seeing Quentin's shining eyes and easy smile, anyone would think he achieved his heart's desire when he took Christabel Urquhart to wife. She'd spoken true when she told him that she didn't deserve him.

CHAPTER NINE

"*S*hall we slip away together now?" Quentin murmured in Kit's ear, as she reached the breathless end of yet another furious reel.

He held her hands after swinging her around so fast that she was dizzy. Or perhaps that was just the effect of staring into his glittering hazel eyes.

Even a girl determined on keeping a level head and remembering the events that led to this riotous frolic hadn't been able to resist the wild joy of the dancing and the genuine happiness that everyone expressed at her marriage to the laird's nephew.

Now Quentin's whispered invitation reminded Kit of their true circumstances and all her giddy excitement shriveled into dread once more. "But the party is for us," she said, looking around the crowded room.

"I think the party has become just a party." Perceptive eyes studied her as she kept a smile plastered to her face. She refused to shame him – and herself – by betraying that her wedding was anything but a love match instead of a complete disaster.

Right now, she'd dearly love to dance down here until new year. In 1850.

Not good enough, Kit.

As always, her cowardice made her cringe. She raised her chin. "Aye, let's go."

"Your ladyship?"

The voice burst the fragile bubble of intimacy that had formed around Kit and Quentin. Kit blinked to break the hold of her new husband's intense gaze. When she released his hand, she struggled against feeling the absence of that sure, steady touch.

"Mrs. McCluskey." Kit searched the housekeeper's face in vain for any hint of resentment for her deception.

The housekeeper, who had been a figure of authority to Kit the stableboy, dipped into a deep curtsy. "I wanted to wish ye and Mr. Quentin a long and happy life together and to say how happy we are downstairs that you've joined the clan."

Kit reached out and caught the middle-aged woman's elbow to help her up. "No, please, I still feel like the lowliest member of the household. You were all so kind to me. I'll always be grateful."

"You never put on airs, my lady. It was an honor to serve ye."

Kit remembered that odd moment on the stairs when Hamish had announced her identity to the household. "You knew all along?"

She should have realized that she wouldn't fool any really sharp eyes. The tact and goodness of the people she'd worked with these last weeks left her floundering.

Mrs. McCluskey smiled with the warm good humor that had such an influence on the atmosphere in Lyon House. "Och, your ladyship, ye did your best, but naebody in their right mind would ever mistake the Countess of Appin for a servant. Or for a lad."

Kit found herself blushing. "Did everyone know?"

"I suspect quite a few of us did. Maybe no' some of the younger ones. They're all silly as wheels."

Quentin caught her hand. Kit told herself that he acted for appearance's sake, but that didn't stop her nitwit heart from breaking into a vigorous jig. Nor did it stop warmth from settling in her stomach where it proved incompatible with her roiling misgivings.

Over the course of the evening, Quentin had often touched her. She had to give him credit for doing a marvelous job of pretending that this wedding was no imposition at all.

"And none of you said anything?" Kit asked.

"I thought a lady of obvious quality must have a good reason for doing such a thing. Now I ken right well that ye did. I'm so sorry ye had to flee your home like that, your ladyship, and I'm proud that here at Glen Lyon we've kept you safe."

A tide of gratitude rose and made tears spring to her eyes. "Thank you from the bottom of my heart."

When Mrs. McCluskey beamed at her, her smile took in Quentin holding Kit's hand. "It was lucky in the end ye came to us, because it meant you met Mr. Quentin."

"Yes, very lucky," she said faintly. "You truly don't mind that I told all those lies?"

"Needs must, my lady. Anyway it's like an old story, ye ken, the runaway countess working as a goose girl and catching the eye of the prince. And to think I was part of it!"

It was Quentin's turn to blush. Bashfulness always looked spectacular on him. Kit was sinkingly aware that everything did. How she wished he'd married her because he wanted to and not because he had to.

Quentin had chosen English clothing for their wedding, but tonight he wore the kilt in the MacNab colours of blue and green. With his snowy white jabot and black velvet coat with its engraved silver buttons, the traditional Highland dress looked magnificent on him.

"Och, away with ye, Mrs. McCluskey. Nobody in their right mind would call me a prince."

Both Kit and the housekeeper spoke in unison. "I would."

Which meant all three laughed.

He regarded the two of them with fond exasperation. "You both talk a lot of nonsense. Now if you'll excuse me, Mrs. McCluskey, I'd like to whisk my goose girl princess of a bride away and keep her to myself for a wee while."

"A wee while?"

Kit blushed even hotter than Quentin had, as he put his arm around her and sent the housekeeper a sly smile. "Perhaps not so wee."

Mrs. McCluskey broke into delighted giggles as Kit surveyed Quentin in admiration. What an actor he was. Anyone would think he was genuinely delighted to marry her.

Luckily a new reel started and the sound of the fiddlers tuning covered Mrs. McCluskey's laughter. Quentin and Kit managed to slip out of the room unnoticed and step into the empty hall, bright with candles.

"It was a bonny way to celebrate our wedding," he said as, keeping hold of her hand, he led her up the main staircase.

Now there was nobody to see them pretend to be joyful newlyweds, Kit supposed she should release his hand. But he didn't seem to have noticed, and she wasn't going to point it out. "It was. These are good people."

"Aye, they are. And it's clear they're fond of you."

"So they should be. I was an excellent stableboy," she said smartly.

Quentin stopped on the first landing and tugged her close for a quick kiss. The contact was over almost before it started. She had a dizzying impression of heat and firm lips before he shifted away.

Kit snatched her hand free and raised it to lips that tingled. "What did you do that for?" she stammered, as her heart performed wild acrobatics in her chest.

He smiled at her as if they remained under observation, even though they were alone here. "Sheer impulse."

"I've never been kissed before."

"Yes, you have. I kissed you when the minister pronounced us man and wife."

He had. A brief brush of his lips across her cheek. It had been even more fleeting than his kiss tonight. But still powerful enough to set her knees wobbling.

"But that wasn't..."

"On the lips?"

"No."

He watched her with a friendly curiosity, as if they discussed something mundane, like whether he took coffee or tea in the morning. "Did you like what I just did?"

Too much.

She raised her chin, scorning the idea of playing coy. "Yes, I did."

When his smile expressed unfettered appreciation, her wayward heart flipped over in her chest. It was doing that a lot tonight. "Well, that's good, then."

"I suppose so," she said in a reedy voice.

Her tone made him bestow a considering look upon her, but to her relief, he didn't keep talking about kisses. He reached out to take her hand again. It was terrifying quite how reassuring she found his touch. Reassuring and disturbing. Because he didn't just touch her now as her defender, but as her husband.

"Actually it's not quite true that I've never been kissed before. Neil's horrid friend tried to kiss me, but I fought him off. I'm stronger than I look."

Quentin frowned. "I hate that those bastards treated you so badly."

"I'm almost free of them."

"Aye, you are. I hope my kisses are nicer than his."

Oh, my... "Definitely."

"I also hope you like my rooms. Hamish and Emily offered us a cottage on the estate, but I thought you might feel safer in the house, at least until your birthday."

"I'm sure I'll love them. Apart from last night, I've been sleeping in a back room in the stables since I arrived. I hardly knew what to do with all the space in the guest bedroom."

He kept hold of her hand as he headed up to the next landing and down a corridor. "How did it feel to be back where you belong?"

"Rather odd. And I've decided skirts are a cursed nuisance."

"As far as I'm concerned, you can wear breeches any time you like."

A short laugh escaped her. "That would shock the tenants at Appin, not to mention the good burghers of Edinburgh."

"Perhaps when we're in private, then. I had no idea until I saw you in boy's clothes how they enhance a shapely female figure. It should become the fashion – except no man in Scotland would do a scrap of work, he'd be too busy looking at the lassies."

"Stuff and nonsense," she said, although a distinctly feminine corner of her soul warmed to know he'd admired her, even when she was a scruffy stableboy.

He came to a halt in front of a closed door. "Here we are."

Here they were.

The nerves that had eased during his silly, teasing conversation coagulated into a frozen ball of terror. She'd fled Appin to avoid wedding a stranger. Yet here she was in Glen Lyon in the very predicament she'd struggled so hard to evade.

Now a wedding night waited on the other side of that door. Kit might like Quentin. She might almost say she trusted Quentin – which felt like a huge concession. But nonetheless she stood on the brink of giving herself to a man, and she was so scared, she was trembling.

Quentin studied her with more of that perception. "You've suddenly gone very green around the gills."

"I...I'm not afraid," she said in a voice that vibrated with dread.

"No, I can see that," he said dryly. "Now hold tight."

"What..." As he swung her up into his arms, she squeaked with shock. "What on earth are you doing?"

"Carrying my lovely bride over the threshold."

She went stiff in his arms, as she fought the urge to curl into his body. He was so deliciously warm, and she felt as if she'd been cold since her father died. "Put me down."

His grip tightened. "Don't you like it?"

"You're acting like this is a real marriage, yet you must know that there's nobody to see."

His smile was gentle. "It felt like a real marriage when Reverend Kinney heard our vows."

"You know what I mean," she said uncomfortably.

"I do. But that doesn't mean I like it. Now put your arm around my neck so I don't drop you. It's the first time I've carried a stableboy. I mightn't have the knack."

Despite everything, a choked giggle rose. "You're a lunatic."

"Undoubtedly."

He jiggled her briefly as he opened the door, then he strode into a candlelit sitting room. The space might have looked dauntingly masculine if it hadn't been decorated with vases of Christmas greenery and flowers from Hamish's heated greenhouses.

"Someone's been busy." Quentin sounded surprised. "This isn't how it looked when I left it."

"It's lovely," Kit said, gazing around in wonder. She was so touched by the efforts everyone had made. Touched and guilty. The clansfolk acted as if this cobbled-together match with Quentin was grounded in true love. "But everyone adores you."

Including me.

"I think they're rather fond of you, too. Shall we investigate the bedroom?"

"Perhaps later," she muttered.

His laugh held more of that breathtaking fondness. "Courage, young Kit. I promise you'll survive to tell the tale."

Kit wasn't convinced, so she took issue with one thing she was sure of. "I'm not that much younger than you are."

"No. That's true."

"You can put me down now, you know," she insisted, because the longer she stayed in his arms, the more she liked it.

"You don't weigh much."

"My big, strong husband."

He laughed and set her on her feet in the center of the festive room. "Let me see what I've caught for myself. We've had such a crowd of people around us all day, I haven't had the chance to take a good look at you."

She blushed as his eyes ate her up and told herself that it couldn't be desire that she read in his face. It was just more consideration for her feelings. He'd been forced into this wedding, and now he did his best to put her at ease.

He really was the prince Mrs. McCluskey had called him. Kit was a lucky girl to be his wife.

She was an unlucky girl, because she wanted so much more from him than he'd ever give her.

"You make a lovely bride, my lady."

She reached up to touch her short hair. "Not a conventional one."

His grunt was dismissive. "Convention is overrated. Now sit down near the fire before you fall down. The green tinge is back."

Kit spread her hands in apology. "I'm sorry."

He smiled at her with such kindness that her poor susceptible heart squeezed painfully tight. Living with her stepbrother, she'd learned the value of kindness, because there had been so little of it.

She'd noticed Quentin's kindness from the first. With animals. With the children. With her.

"A few bridal nerves are *de rigueur*, I believe."

"A few?"

But all the same, she didn't feel quite as jittery when she sank into a leather chair in front of the blazing hearth. If only because it seemed that her bridegroom wasn't about to rush her into bed and have his way with her this very minute.

"Here. This might help." He came to stand in front of her with two crystal glasses in his hands. He held one out. "Bruce Mackenzie's finest."

She knew about Bruce Mackenzie, the best whisky distiller in the Highlands, who lived on the Achnasheen estate over on the coast. Her fellow stablehands had spoken of his product with awe.

"You know I don't like spirits."

"I had a feeling you were developing a taste for them in the hut. Try some now. It might fire up your courage."

She didn't take the glass. "Do I need to fire up my courage?"

"A bit of extra courage never goes astray."

"That's true." She reached out to take the glass, sure Quentin wouldn't miss how unsteady her hand was.

"*Slàinte mhath.*" He drank the whisky in one gulp.

"*Slàinte mhath,*" she echoed and cautiously sipped the golden liquid. It had such a strong taste, she couldn't help grimacing, although at least this time, she knew what to expect.

"You'll get used to it," Quentin said on a laugh.

"It still tastes like medicine." She felt a lovely heat now she'd swallowed it, and the aftertaste wasn't unpleasant at all, rich and peaty and smoky.

As she took another sip, Quentin turned away to set his glass on the mantel. The taste became more palatable.

She watched him cross to the desk under the curtained windows. He returned with a piece of paper that he held out in her direction.

"This is for you."

Puzzled, she set her glass on the table near her chair and reached to take it. "What is this?"

"It relinquishes any claim I might make on your fortune." For once, his voice held no hint of teasing. "I told you I'd do this. We can go to Edinburgh in the New Year and have a lawyer draw up something official. But I've signed this and I had the minister witness it, so I suspect it will hold up in a court."

Bewildered, she read the few lines on the sheet of paper and felt sick as she did so. "I'd almost feel better if you did take control of my property."

"What the devil?"

Kit swallowed to shift the massive lump of dismay and guilt in her throat. And longing. When she was with Quentin, longing was always paramount.

She raised a bleak gaze to him. "At least if you kept my fortune, I'd feel you got something out of this marriage."

With those words, all the spun sugar illusion of her wedding day dissolved to nothing.

Yet Quentin frowned as if he didn't understand. "I get something out of this marriage. I get you."

She made a despairing gesture, and her voice was toneless as she fought not to cry. "Stop being kind, Quentin. We both know you were cornered into this wedding. You'd never have done it, if you hadn't had to."

She braced to hear him protest about what she said. Right now, she didn't think she could bear more of his kindness.

But instead of giving her another comforting lie, he bent his head and stared into the flames. When he spoke, his tone was somber as she'd never heard it before. "I know you didn't want to marry me."

It wasn't what she'd expected him to say, so surprise made her respond with more candor than perhaps was wise. "Don't be a blockhead, Quentin. Of course I wanted to marry you. You're wonderful."

His head jerked up, and he went white with shock. Which seemed an odd reaction. "Wonderful?"

She released a grim little laugh. "I've been mooning around after you since the day I first saw you. It was most unbecoming behavior in a stableboy."

He spread his hands in confusion, for once lost for words. "I…"

She signaled him to silence. "But I hate that you were trapped into taking me as your wife. You deserve better."

He shook his head, and that chiseled jaw set with stubbornness. "No, I don't."

She battled tears. Crying right now would be the last straw. "I told you not to be kind."

"I'm not."

"Yes, you are. And don't worry, I won't embarrass you by making scenes or letting my fondness for you become an issue. Once we've seen Neil off, we can separate. You can go on with your life as if I don't exist."

A muscle jerked in his cheek, and he looked annoyed. Which was odd, because she thought he'd be grateful that she made it so easy for him to ignore his obligations to his bride. "Except you're my wife."

"I'm sorry. I can't change that. I would if I could."

Skeptical eyebrows rose. "Would you indeed?"

Quentin had stopped looking quite so devastated, she noticed, although she supposed her unwelcome confession meant he now felt sorry for her. This evening slid into a complete debacle.

"For your sake."

"How very...self-sacrificing."

He still sounded annoyed. She supposed the revelation that his unwanted wife harbored a penchant for him must come as a nasty surprise.

Not really understanding what he wanted from her, she made a helpless gesture. "I wish I could set you free."

"Aye?"

Actually he was right to doubt her. Kit wasn't sure she was quite so noble, although she wished she was. It was absurd to hope, but hope she did. Perhaps Quentin might learn to want her in time. Perhaps he might come to care.

"I'm sorry I blighted your life," she said in a low miserable voice.

Without moving from the mantel, he studied her the way he'd studied her before he announced that he knew she was a girl. She shifted uncomfortably on the chair. When he stared at her like this, she felt like he saw right to her heart. And she was humiliatingly aware that her heart carried an image of his face.

"Well, this is a surprise," he said in a neutral voice after a long silence.

She couldn't help feeling that he was toying with her. Her response emerged with a hint of a snap. "I can't help what I feel."

He went on as if she hadn't spoken. "Because I've spent the last two days convinced I've blighted your life."

Actually the prospect of a lifetime of unrequited love could fit that description. But she met his eyes as bravely as she could. "I'm proud to be your wife."

To her relief, his stern expression lightened. "And I'm proud to be your husband."

"You...you are?"

"Aye, with all my heart." His eyes warmed, as his lips curved into a smile. "Because you see, I'm very happy to marry you, Christabel Urquhart. I'm even happier now that I know you're not averse to the idea either."

She frowned, as she struggled to make sense of how the world had changed in these last few seconds. "Are you saying..."

His smile broadened. "I'm saying that if the stableboy was looking inappropriately lovelorn, so was the laird's nephew."

A frail seedling of hope unfurled in her chest. This sounded promising. It did indeed. Perhaps the day wasn't proving such a disaster after all. Lovelorn mightn't be love, but it was a good start.

"Are you...are you saying you're content with how things have turned out?"

"I'm saying that there's nobody I'd rather spend the rest of my life with. What made me feel as low as a snake's belly was that I was sure my damned curiosity meant you'd been forced into marrying me, when it was the last thing you wanted."

The seedling of hope stretched toward the light. "We...we seem to have been mistaken in each other."

He kept watching her, as if he saw every breath she took. "We do."

She seized her courage in both hands and met his burning gaze. "So what are we going to do about it?"

CHAPTER TEN

Quentin had spent the last two days racked between lacerating guilt for snaring Kit in this marriage and unworthy happiness that he'd caught the girl he wanted.

Now it turned out his happiness wasn't so unworthy after all. Because it seemed the girl he wanted wanted him, too.

It was all too huge a change for his mind to encompass. So when his lovely bride asked him what he intended to do, he spoke of his most immediate concern. "What I'd like to do is take my wife to bed."

Shining blue eyes widened, and he rushed to continue before she could send him to the devil. Or run out of the room, shrieking in terror. "But I'm well aware that you hardly know me and we had no opportunity to court, so if you'd like to wait, I understand."

When Kit licked her lips, he closed his eyes and reminded himself he was a gentleman. He also reminded himself that she'd been bullied and mistreated. He owed it to her to let her set the timetable for her seduction.

At least there was some satisfaction now in knowing that there would indeed be a seduction. He opened his eyes to catch her watching him.

"That's very generous," she said, her expression unreadable.

He smiled. "I'm a prince after all. Ask Mrs. McCluskey."

"I don't need to." She stood up and approached him. "Will you kiss me, Quentin?"

Surprise shuddered through him. And anticipation. This sounded promising.

"I'd love to."

She stopped about a foot away. This close, he read the nervousness swirling beneath her bravado. But he already knew she was brave. If she wasn't, she'd have buckled under her stepbrother's tyranny, instead of defying him by running away disguised as a boy.

Christabel Urquhart, now MacNab, was so strong, but she was also vulnerable. He felt a surge of protectiveness as he gazed into her exquisite face. The vows he'd spoken this morning took on a new weight. While he lived, he wouldn't let anyone hurt her.

His touch was tender as he caught her face in one hand and tilted her chin up. At the contact, her breath caught and her eyes darkened, but she didn't pull away.

Slowly he lowered his head and brushed his lips across hers. Swift heat enveloped him, although the contact was chaste and over in a second.

Quentin took a grip on his wilder impulses and gave her another of those glancing kisses. Her lips were so soft, full and pillowy under his. He resisted the urge to sink into the kiss and drink his full of her sweetness.

Kit gave a murmur of pleasure and shifted closer. Encouraged, the next time he kissed her, he lingered, taking a moment extra to savor her taste. With the following kiss, her lips moved beneath his with the beginnings of response.

He sucked her lush lower lip into his mouth, inviting her to open to him. When she made a faint sound of bewilderment, he retreated.

"You didn't like that?" he whispered, lifting his other hand so he cradled her face.

Her cheeks were pink, and the heaviness in her gaze told him this gradual wooing achieved its aims. "It was unexpected. That's all."

"Shall I do it again?"

"Yes, please," she sighed and closed her eyes as she lifted her face.

He went back to gentle kisses. When he flicked his tongue across the closed seam of her lips, instead of withdrawing this time, she parted to let him in. Fighting a surge of triumph, he slipped his tongue into the honeyed interior.

She made another of those soft sounds of surrender and the next time his tongue slid into her mouth, she dared to meet him with a flutter of hers.

He groaned and released her face so he could curl his arms around her and haul her against his shaking body. Because this careful seduction seduced him, too. Gentleness became harder to maintain when she twined her arms around him and pressed closer. She was vital and slender in his embrace and each time he kissed her, it became more of a battle not to plunder her mouth with all the passion rising inside him.

His kisses remained playful, although it was a struggle to remember her innocence, her fragility. He'd cut his throat before he let himself frighten her. She'd already been frightened enough.

Quentin raised his head and stared down at Kit through dazed eyes. She looked all rosy and befuddled, and he'd never seen anything more beautiful in his life.

A faint frown drew those winged brows together. "Why did you stop?"

"Because I'm trying to keep my head, and you're so beguiling, it's not easy."

He laughed when she looked mighty pleased with herself. "I liked kissing you."

"I liked kissing you, too." A sudden uncomfortable thought struck him. "Do you know what happens between a man and a woman?"

By God, he hoped so, or he feared that he'd frighten her again.

The sardonic look she cast him was so much Kit, the insubordinate stableboy, that he laughed again. "I grew up around horses. I understand the basics."

"With people, it's not quite the same as a stallion mounting a mare."

She made a face that made him want to kiss her again. "I hope not. The mare never seems to enjoy it very much."

He remained caught between concern and amusement. "I'm not sure a woman enjoys her first time either. Although I don't speak from experience."

"But you have done this before?"

As her gaze sharpened on him, he blushed. "Kit..."

"I'm not supposed to ask that, am I?"

He caught her hand, as he remembered bonny Jenny McLeod, the jolliest widow this side of the border, who had turned his twentieth summer to magic. Here with Kit, he had difficulty recalling

Jenny's face. "Perhaps not, but, aye, I have done this before."

Jenny had taken a raw, eager boy and taught him how to give and receive pleasure. The next year, she'd married a spice merchant and now lived in Glasgow. He hoped that she was happy. She'd certainly made Quentin happy for a couple of sunlit months.

Kit's voice remained serious. "Emily talked to me about what happens. She said if the lover is kind, even the first time can be glorious."

Quentin wasn't sure he wanted quite so much insight into his aunt and uncle's marital life, although anyone could see that the love they shared included a healthy portion of physical enjoyment. "That gives me an awful lot to live up to."

She smiled. "If...if you mean it when you say you'd like to make this a real marriage between us, we've got time to get it right."

"Lots of practice ahead?"

It was her turn to blush. "I...I hope so. If what is to come is anything like kissing you, I won't complain."

He smothered the thought of having Kit in his bed for hours on end. Right now he needed control, and that idea was a sure way to snap his restraint.

"I'll do my best," he said, smiling at her. "And I do want to make this a real marriage. I want to live with you and fight your battles and grow old at your side. What do you say?"

Kit's grip on his hand tightened. "So you're not angry at all that we had to marry?"

He shook his head. "I want you, Kit. I hadn't worked out how I'd manage it, but I had intentions of courting you."

"The laird's nephew and the stableboy?"

"Sounds absurd, doesn't it?" He went on to mention something that niggled at him. "Although a union between a mere laird and a countess sounds absurd, too. You could look much higher than me for a husband."

She studied him as if she saw right to his heart. "You know, there is more to a laddie than his title. You're a good man, Quentin MacNab. In every way that counts, I could look no higher than you."

"You don't know me."

Her huff of amusement expressed utter contempt for that statement. "Of course I do. I've seen how you treat children and horses and dogs. I've seen how you treat Hamish and Emily. When we spent that night in the hut, I know that you were a perfect knight in shining armor. If you had any designs on my fortune, you had me at your mercy then. Yet I slept in your arms in complete safety."

He lifted her hand to kiss her knuckles. "I have no designs on your fortune. I do however have designs on your person."

"Why didn't you try and kiss me at the hut?"

He shrugged. "Because you weren't ready. Because you were afraid. Because you didn't yet trust me."

"I trust you now," she said softly.

The words sounded like a declaration of love. Given what Kit had been through, trust was perhaps a greater gift than love, which didn't mean that Quentin harbored no hopes of making her love him one day.

"Enough to become my wife in every sense?"

For the first time, she gave him a smile without shadows. She reached up to stroke his cheek. He was sharply conscious that she'd never before touched him of her own initiative. A physical expression of the trust she pledged in words.

"I can't wait."

CHAPTER ELEVEN

When Kit saw hunger flare in Quentin's hazel eyes, turning them vivid gold, giddy anticipation flooded her. She'd been afraid for so long, but staring into her husband's intense features, she wasn't afraid now.

"Kit..."

He swept her into his arms for a kiss so sizzling that it cast his earlier kisses, thrilling as they'd been, into the shade. When he sucked her tongue into his mouth, heat overwhelmed her. As her knees threatened to crumple, she clutched at his broad shoulders.

He began to kiss her face and neck. Sensation rippled through her and made her cry out when he concentrated on a particularly sensitive spot where her neck joined her shoulder. These unfamiliar reactions turned her body into a stranger's. Her breasts swelled, and her nipples tightened to aching neediness. Her stomach clenched with restless yearning.

"Quentin, I feel so odd," she choked out.

He raised his head and stared down at her. He too looked like a stranger. An alluring, dangerous stranger. But his voice was full of familiar kindness. "Good or bad odd?"

"Good." Although her essential honesty made her add, "I think."

The soft laugh that always made her heart melt soothed her disquiet. "You're meant to feel that way."

When he stepped back, she made an incoherent protest and caught his arms, too stirred up for pride. "Don't stop."

He smoothed her short hair back from her face and gave her a smile of surpassing sweetness. "I won't stop. In fact, I'm planning much more."

Half an hour ago, that might have daunted her. Now his words only sparked a rush of excitement. "This isn't like horses."

He laughed again. "No, not entirely. May I undress you?"

The breath whooshed out of her lungs so fast that she saw spots in front of her eyes. "If...if you'd like to," she managed to squeak out.

"Thank you."

She braced for him to start removing her clothes, but instead he stepped back and unbuttoned his black velvet coat and shrugged it off, tossing it over the back of the chair near the fire. When he untied his neck cloth, she noticed his hands were shaking. Then with increasing urgency, he tugged his loose white shirt over his head. Neck cloth and shirt joined the coat over the chair.

"Oh, my..." she sighed, as her gaze devoured his bare chest.

At Appin, she'd seen the grooms and fieldworkers without their shirts. Here at Glen Lyon, a stableboy was exposed to a masculine world no countess ever entered, despite Laing's best efforts to protect her. None of those men could compare to Quentin MacNab's magnificence.

As she surveyed her husband, every drop of moisture dried from her mouth and her stomach tightened with more of that painful longing. "May I...may I touch you?" she stammered, eating up the sight of that powerful chest with its light covering of tawny hair.

She'd never noticed before the way that hard muscles formed ridges over a masculine abdomen. Quentin looked strong and deliciously appealing.

A faint smile curled his lips. "I'd like that."

She placed unsteady hands in the center of his chest. His hair was a pleasant prickle under her palms. At the contact, he inhaled on a long hiss.

She raised an uncertain gaze to his. "Is this all right?"

"Och, aye."

Encouraged, she spread her hands. He was so warm. Heat radiated up her arms and sizzled down through her body to that place in the pit of her stomach where she felt empty and needy. She bit her lip as she slowly discovered the hard ribs and firm belly and finally the flat brown nipples that peaked under her touch, just as hers did when he kissed her.

This close, she heard his ragged breathing. When she touched his nipples, he stopped breathing altogether. Tentatively she rubbed them, and he released a broken groan.

"You're torturing me."

He didn't sound like he minded too much. With sudden daring, she leaned forward and kissed the middle of his chest. His scent enveloped her, familiar after the night in the hut and his kisses tonight. Herbal soap. Healthy male. Something musky that her instincts told her was arousal.

"You smell wonderful," she murmured into his skin.

He caught her head between his hands and tipped her face up for another kiss, this one clumsy with need. She slid her hands up his chest and linked them behind his neck, as she met him with every ounce of the untried passion that turned her blood to flame.

When he raised his head, he stared down at her with an expression that thrilled her. He looked as if he was just as overwhelmed by the fire rising between them as she was. "I'm trying not to frighten you."

She smiled. "I'm not frightened."

"I'm glad. I never want you to be frightened when you're with me." He smiled back. "Will you turn around so I can unlace your dress?"

With no hesitation, she shifted to present her back. Emily had lent her a beautiful cream velvet gown for the wedding. "It would be easier to undress me if I was still a stableboy."

He gave a grunt of amusement, as he tugged at the fastenings with an impatience she could feel. "Even the unconventional Countess of Appin couldn't get married in breeches." He paused. "And with you looking so lovely standing by my side in front of the minister, it would be ungracious to complain about needing time to undress you."

"I thought you looked lovely, too."

"Thank you."

When humor deepened his voice, she blushed. She supposed that lovely wasn't the best word to use to describe a handsome young man.

"The MacNab kilt looked spectacular on you. I wish I could have worn the Urquhart tartan."

"I'm sorry it was such a small wedding. I know girls dream of the crowded church and the elaborate dress and a hundred bridesmaids. My dashed sisters talked of little else, well before any of them decided which poor sod to marry."

Kit gave a self-derisive snort. "I didn't dream of getting married. I dreamed of breeding a Derby winner."

She released a startled gasp, as he whirled her around and kissed her again. By the time he raised his head, she was breathless and dizzy.

"What was that for?" she gasped, clinging to his shoulders, so she didn't dissolve into a puddle at his feet.

He smiled at her as if he'd never seen anything so wonderful. "That's for you being you. I'm so happy you married me."

She stared into his face and for the first time believed in her heart that while the threat of scandal might have compelled them to wed, he wasn't an unwilling bridegroom.

"And I'm happy you married me." She went on in a rush. "I don't care that it was just you and me and Hamish and Emily and Laing at the wedding. What matters is that you promised to be mine and I promised to be yours. Because I meant those words with all my heart."

His expression changed, and she saw that her words left him profoundly moved. "Christabel, I don't deserve you."

Wondering, she stared up at him. "You've never called me that before."

He touched her cheek with such tenderness that she felt ready to melt. "Tonight you're Christabel, beautiful and mysterious."

She'd never before felt that her prosaic, busy self measured up to such a fanciful name, but as she stared into Quentin's blazing gold eyes, for the first time rough-and-tumble Kit was also Christabel.

"You make me Christabel," she whispered.

He smiled and touched her hair. "Although I hope Kit's still in there somewhere. I'd miss that ragamuffin if I never saw her again."

His teasing leavened the intense atmosphere building between them, and she laughed. "I promise Kit will be back."

"Excellent news. I did so enjoy kissing a stableboy."

A stifled giggle emerged. "That would have caused a scandal indeed."

"Now let me see what Kit was hiding under that execrable coat," Quentin said, letting her go and moving behind her again to finish untying her laces. "The thought has kept me awake for many a night."

Now that was nice to hear. "Has it indeed?"

"Oh, yes."

She gulped. He kept saying these things that stole her breath. "The coat was a bit of an eyesore, wasn't it?"

He gave a grunt of sardonic laughter. "An eyesore? It was uglier than a two-headed pig."

"I'll burn it."

"Don't you dare. It holds wonderful memories for me. Not to mention that I want to show it to our children when I tell them about their mother's adventures."

"Ch...children?" It seemed absurd, but until now Kit hadn't really considered bearing Quentin's children. Life in recent years had been a series of short-term decisions, made in a rush to solve a current crisis. She'd barely had the chance to look beyond the next week.

"Of course."

"Of course," she said on a breath.

His tone remained teasing. "How do you feel about half a dozen?"

Something inside her twisted with poignant emotion. He'd make a good father. She had a sudden vivid image of a little boy with Quentin's mussed tawny hair and bright hazel eyes and arresting intelligence.

Thanks to Quentin – and Hamish and Emily and Laing, too – her long ordeal was nearly over. One more day, and she was free of Neil. In fact, in marrying Quentin, she was free now. The terms of her father's will were that once she wed, she gained control of her inheritance.

The constant tension loosened, and the next breath she took filled her lungs in a way no breath had, since long before her father's death. "Let's start with one and see how we go from there," she said, struggling to keep her voice even.

"Sounds like a plan. Lift your arms."

Without thinking – she was too preoccupied imagining the future that extended before her – she did. Quentin pulled the pretty dress over her head and crossed to lay it over the chair. He took considerably more care with her clothes that he had with his own, she noticed.

As he walked, the kilt swayed about his narrow hips. He was surely naked beneath the plaid. At the thought, her heart leaped with a mixture of excitement and trepidation. "You make a fine lady's maid."

He returned to her, still with that graceful swinging gait. "I intend to spend a lot of time undressing my wife."

She flushed, as she suddenly realized that she stood in front of him wearing only her undergarments. Before this, she'd been too busy admiring the fine figure of a man she'd married to notice.

When he paused in front of her, the blatant admiration in his gaze made her cheeks burn hotter. "By heaven, that dreadful coat covered buried treasure."

He reached forward to unhook her corset and draw it away, leaving her in shift and petticoats. Emily had lent her everything she wore, not just the elaborate wedding gown. Emily, it turned out, had a fondness for naughty, extravagant undergarments. Embroidered birds and branches twined around the pale pink corset, and the shift and petticoats were sheer white silk.

Quentin's hands worked fast as he untied the tapes on her petticoats, until they slithered to the floor at her feet. Kit might still wear shift and drawers and stockings and slippers, but she felt close to naked. Under his hungry gaze, she shifted self-consciously, even as her breasts ached for the touch of his hands.

Gently he drew her forward and kissed her again. Despite her innocence, she sensed a universe of hunger banked behind the kiss. Her knees turned to jelly, and she slid one hand behind his neck to keep her balance. And to touch him. Touching Quentin turned out to be one of life's greatest delights.

Kissing her, he began to investigate her shape through the fine material. Running his hands up and down her back, spanning her waist, stroking the bare skin of her arms. Her nervousness receded under the wash of pleasure. When he lowered his hands to squeeze her buttocks, she made a soft sound of surprise against his seeking mouth. Then another gasp as he pulled her against his thighs.

She felt his hardness through his kilt. Hot liquid welled in the pit of her stomach, and she shifted at the unfamiliar craving.

Quentin wrenched up the hem of her shift and released her drawers, so they fell about her ankles with her petticoats. He made a soft growl of satisfaction as this time his hands closed around the naked cheeks of her bottom. A shudder of response rushed through her and made her whimper.

"Come into the bedroom, my lovely wife," he whispered, trailing his lips along her neck.

Anticipation rushed through her, and goose bumps broke out all over her skin. "Aye," she said shakily.

He kissed her softly on the lips. Earlier he'd seemed all impatience, but now every touch conveyed care and tenderness. Taking her hand, he led her through the doorway into the candlelit bedroom. A fire roared in the hearth, so even wearing as little as she did, she was warm.

"How very pretty," she said. More flowers and Christmas greenery decorated the room, and fragrant flower petals were scattered across the sheets and pillows. Bowls of herbs were placed around the room, so the air smelled like paradise. "They've gone to such trouble for us."

"Everyone is overjoyed to welcome you to the family."

Kit blinked back tears. "I feel like I haven't had a family for so long. Since Papa died, it's been like living with a pack of wolves."

"I'm your family now," Quentin said softly, as he drew her close for a swift kiss that was all gentleness.

Powerful emotion squeezed her heart. Of all the lovely things he'd said tonight, this was the most moving. "Thank you. You can't know what that means to me."

"I can guess."

Her free hand made a gesture eloquent of her past unhappiness. "I've felt so alone since Papa died. Which sounds ungrateful, when Emily and Hamish and Laing have done so much to help me."

"That isn't the same as having someone of your own."

"You understand."

"I think so." His voice deepened in a way that had her unruly heart cramping again. "I won't let you feel lost and alone ever again, Christabel. You have my word as a MacNab on it."

She swallowed to shift the painful tightness in her throat. Then again. Yet her answer still emerged as a husky rasp. "Then I think it's time you made me a MacNab in truth, Quentin."

CHAPTER TWELVE

Quentin drew Christabel into his arms and kissed her with more of the aching tenderness she aroused in him. But it seemed that his bride had moved beyond the trembling uncertainty that called on his gentleness. Her response was hungry, summoning up the desire he was doing his best to leash.

He wanted to cherish her, show her how much he valued her, but she wound her arms around his neck and tugged at his hair and arched her body against his until he felt the beaded crests of her nipples against his chest. He cupped her breasts through their sheer covering. The silk was slippery under his hands, tightening on the points of her nipples. Her figure was lusher than he'd realized when he'd studied the self-effacing stableboy and guessed that Kit was no male, but a girl in disguise.

With a sigh of satisfaction, he squeezed the soft flesh and bent his head to take one sweet, silk-covered point between his lips. Kit released a broken cry of surprised pleasure and sagged in his hold. He drew on the tip as he caressed her other breast, then lifted his head. Her face was flushed, and her lips were red and full. Her eyelids were heavy over dark blue eyes. She was the perfect image of female surrender.

He glanced down to where damp silk outlined one pink nipple. The pale material clung to the curve of her hip and hinted at the glorious mysteries between her legs. Suddenly even this transparent garment provided too much concealment. He needed to see her body.

With shaking hands, he caught her shift and tugged it over her head, letting it drift to the ground behind her. Then he lost the ability to speak.

Hell, he lost the ability to breathe.

"Quentin..." she stammered, hands fluttering at her sides.

He knew she was desperate to cover herself, but he reached out and caught her wrists to stop her. She was lithe and slender, and her skin was as white as snow, so the rich raspberry nipples and the feathery dark curls that covered her sex were shocking in their erotic color. She was trembling, and she jerked in his hold, as though she still wanted to restore her modesty.

He'd imagined her naked, of course he had. Far too often to save him from feeling like a lustful satyr. But the reality of his bride's unclothed body beggared even the most spectacular of his dreams.

It took an almighty effort, but Quentin mustered a few gruff words. "You're beyond beautiful."

"Thank you," she said, with those perfect manners he'd noticed from the first as so incongruous in a mere stableboy.

The reminder made him smile. "It's my pleasure, believe me."

She smiled back with touching uncertainty, and she stopped trying to pull away. This expression of trust made his heart turn over with gratitude and more of that almost agonizing protectiveness. "Let me touch you," he murmured.

Wide eyes fixed on his features, and she licked her lips. But she nodded. Another concession. "I'd like that."

Her bravery, when it was clear she was drowning in shyness, sliced at his heart. After he released her hands, his touch was light when he brushed along her shoulders and down her slender arms. Catching her hands, he brought them briefly to his lips. He placed swift kisses on her knuckles, then turned them over to kiss her palms with more lingering attention, until her eyelids fluttered and she curved toward him.

He shaped her flanks and hips and finally held her bare breasts, his thumbs flicking at the crests until she gasped. Only then did he lean in and put his mouth on her, suckling and using his tongue and teeth to drive her wild.

She clung to his shoulders and pressed forward in quivering encouragement. Her flowery scent rose to tempt him. Drawing hard on her nipple, he finally dared to touch her between the legs. She was wet and sleek beneath his exploring fingers and lusciously hot. He stroked the delicate folds and found the place that made a woman quake.

Her shuddering gasp made him swell against the soft plaid of his kilt. He'd been hard since they'd started kissing, but touching her naked body rushed him toward the moment when he needed to be inside her. He scraped his teeth across her nipple, as he teased her center of pleasure until she was shaking.

"What...what wonderful things you're doing to me," she muttered, holding his head to her breasts and jutting her hips forward.

"There's more," he murmured against her skin and raised his head. He caught her around the waist and swung her until she tumbled against the sheets. Coming down over her, he reveled in the eager way her arms curled around him. He kissed her with open-mouthed fervor. "I need to take off this damned kilt."

She let him go and shifted up against the pillows, reaching down to remove her stockings and cream satin slippers. "I'd like to see you."

He rose to his knees and with fumbling hands unbuckled the black leather belt. Then he quickly pushed away the kilt, so that he was bare to her gaze.

She gave a muffled squeak, and her gaze was wide and wondering as it focused on the hard flesh rising between his thighs.

"What are you thinking about?"

To his surprise, eyes bright with laughter met his. She looked breathtakingly like the faux stableboy who had captured his interest. "Horses."

He started to laugh, then couldn't wait any longer. He surged forward and caught her in his arms, kissing her with mad abandon. He'd imagined it would take all night to coax his bride into accepting his possession – if she accepted him at all. But with a sweetness that surpassed imagination, he found himself poised between her thighs, ready to thrust into her.

"Christabel?" he asked on a long, broken exhalation.

She stared up at him, eyes weighty with need. "Make me your wife, Quentin. I'm ready."

He slid his hand along her cleft and discovered that she was, as she said, ready. He pushed one finger inside her. By God, she was tight. All the time, he watched her face.

When discomfort drew her sleek black brows together, he stopped. "Does that hurt?"

"No."

"But you don't like it?"

As Kit shifted, her grip on his finger firmed. "I'm just not used to it."

"It will help prepare you for when I'm inside you," he said in a thick voice.

She hooked her hands over his shoulders and raised her knees. He kissed her again and while his tongue was inside her mouth, he began to move his finger in and out in a rhythm that echoed what his body would soon do to her. He felt her tension ease, and her face flushed with rising pleasure. When he tried two fingers, she took him more readily.

"I want...I want you," she said in a constricted voice, digging her fingers into the muscles of his arms. "Don't make me wait. This is like standing on the edge of a cliff."

Quentin knew what she meant. The need to possess her was driving him insane. He kissed her again, hard and with carnal intent. Then he tightened his hips and edged forward. Kit gasped as he entered her, then bit back a strangled cry and jerked toward him as he inched further.

He made himself stop, although the snug clasp of her body made his blood clamor to fill her full-length. "I hurt you," he said with a universe of regret, even as his animal self gloried in being inside her.

"A little. The sting is already going away."

She settled more deeply into the mattress, and the change in angle threatened to make his head explode. He groaned. "I'm sorry, Kit. I'll try and make it better for you."

"Don't stop," she gasped.

This time, when she shifted to accommodate his thickness, she released a moan that sounded more like pleasure than pain. Carefully he shifted, until she'd taken all of him. Staring into her eyes, he felt like he saw right to her soul. This joining changed him forever. He and this woman established a union that would endure the rest of their lives.

"Oh, yes," she said on a soft hiss. When she tightened around him, he saw stars.

"Do that...do that again," he growled.

She looked startled. "Do what?"

"You...hugged me inside." It was an inadequate description, but it was the best he could manage.

Her eyes turned opaque, as she squeezed him again. He struggled not to lose himself. If he could manage it, he wanted to show her pleasure.

Gritting his teeth, he pulled back, savoring every fraction of his withdrawal. He thrust again and watched her eyes widen.

"That was..."

"Good?" Dear God, don't let him mistake what he read in her expression.

"Better than good."

"I'll do it again."

True to his word, he began to move, feeling each tiny adjustment she made for him, until there was nothing but hot welcome. He relished the soft sounds of delight she made as he claimed her. When she rose to meet him with untamed eagerness, pride burgeoned in his heart. The sighs and moans and whimpers combined into a symphony of surrender. He watched her face change, as she climbed toward her peak.

"Don't fight it, Kit." The next time he thrust into her, he reached down between her legs. She released a breathy cry and shuddered across into ecstasy. She clenched tight around him. He shifted in and out once more, then gave himself up to her with a shuddering groan.

She was shaking when he slumped exhausted on top of her, burying his face in her shoulder. Through his blissful languor, he felt her caress his hair with a tenderness that made his heart ache.

"My wife," he said in a hoarse voice.

"Yes, your wife," Kit whispered and wrapped her arms around him, holding him close to her naked body.

CHAPTER THIRTEEN

The Christmas Eve ball at Lyon House was in full swing. Kit glanced around as Quentin led her onto the floor for their second waltz of the night. People had gathered from all over the Highlands for the elegant event. She'd met so many of Hamish and Emily's friends and neighbors and family, she'd completely lost track of who everyone was. Not that her mind was on anyone except her handsome bridegroom in his black velvet coat and plaid kilt, the same clothes he'd worn at their wedding ceilidh yesterday.

The ball had transformed into a celebration to mark their marriage. Now midnight approached and the moment she turned twenty-one. She was almost free of Neil, and she was married to the man she wanted. Even better, it turned out that Quentin wanted her, too. After so many years of fear and unhappiness, she could hardly believe that such joy existed. For so long, she'd been afraid to hope, but tonight at the most joyous season of the year, hope rose in an invincible tide.

Quentin smiled at her. He'd smiled at her all night, as if he could hardly believe his luck that she was his wife. Any doubt she'd had that this was purely a marriage of convenience had long faded. After their glorious hours together last night, she was convinced that their union had begun just right, and the bond they built between them would only strengthen as the years went on.

Perhaps she already carried the next MacNab heir. If she didn't, it wasn't for want of trying. Warmth flooded her, as she recalled Quentin's passion and gentleness last night – not to mention twice this morning before they made a late appearance at the breakfast table. Then before they dressed for the ball, he'd done his husbandly duty once more.

"If you keep looking at me like that, you won't be downstairs when the clock strikes midnight," Quentin growled, sweeping her into his arms for a dizzying turn as the lilting music swelled. Around them, the dance floor was crowded with couples dressed in the height of fashion. The ladies sparkled with jewels, and the men were resplendent in their vivid plaids.

Kit had never had a season, although she'd had dancing lessons in preparation for one. Waltzing in Appin Castle's ballroom with a stout dancing master, while her governess thumped out a tune on the pianoforte, couldn't compare to swirling around amidst a glittering crowd, while the man she loved held her in his arms.

She gave him a saucy smile that she'd never have managed a day ago. "I don't mind."

"It would be a pity to miss out on marking the moment when you're finally out of Neil's control."

"I've been out of Neil's control since I married you."

"Doubly free, then."

"I'm almost grateful that Neil was such a swine," she said, her voice bubbling with teasing humor.

"That can't be true." Quentin's hands tightened on her waist, as he brought her too near for propriety. But most of the couples around them danced in close embrace, including Hamish and Emily. Kit said a silent prayer that her marriage to Quentin thrived like theirs.

Her smile broadened. She'd been grinning like a cat with the cream all night. So had Quentin. She'd caught frequent looks of indulgent amusement, as the other guests noticed her bedazzlement.

"Oh, it is," she said solemnly, daring to slide her hand along his shoulder to caress his earlobe. "Unless Neil had tormented me into running away, I'd never have met you. That would be a crying shame."

She watched his expression soften. Then she saw nothing but stars when he kissed her quickly. "In that case, we must call our first child Neil."

She grimaced, hardly believing that she felt safe enough to joke about the man who had made her life such a misery. "That might be a step too far." She paused, too elated to stew on past unhappiness. "Especially if our firstborn is a girl."

Quentin laughed, drawing a few more of those knowing glances. "Fair point." He surveyed her. "You made a very pretty stableboy, my Lady Appin. But you make a spectacular countess."

Self-consciously, she released his shoulder to fiddle with her coiffure. "I still feel like a bit of a freak with such short hair."

As he swept her into another breathtaking turn, Quentin's smile was redolent with a tenderness that made her feel like the most cherished woman in the world. "It will grow again if you want it long, but I've heard quite a few of the ladies say they rather fancy a countess crop themselves. You're setting the style."

With a self-derisive huff, she curled her hand around his shoulder again. She so loved dancing with Quentin. It was the closest to flying she could come without growing wings.

Although tonight she was euphoric enough to feel like she could take off into the sky without the need of wings.

"Perhaps I should have worn my stableboy's jacket. That would have really got them talking about a new fashion."

Wry humor lengthened Quentin's mouth. "Tonight's gown is a definite improvement on that monstrosity."

She glanced down at the gorgeous emerald silk dress with its elaborate gold braiding. "It's another one courtesy of Emily. It will be nice to wear my own clothes again."

"Once we settle things at Appin, we can do a honeymoon trip, if you like. I plan to take you to Cannich House, too, so you can meet my family." He smiled at her. "Don't look so bilious. They'll love you."

"I'm not a conventional daughter-in-law," she said, knowing that was an understatement.

"No, you're better than that. My grandmother in particular will adore you. She's a famous political hostess in London. We'll have to visit her as well. Which means you can go wild in the West End shops."

"You...you seem to have it all worked out," she said faintly, feeling overwhelmed.

"I'm proud of my new bride. I want to show her off."

"It all sounds rather daunting." Especially the bit about meeting his family. "I've lived a very quiet life, you know."

He gave a snort. "Apart from your adventures as a stableboy."

"Those aren't likely to recommend me to a mother-in-law."

When his smile warmed, a glow settled in her stomach. "It will to this particular mother-in-law. We're not precisely a conventional family either. Hamish and Emily are outside the normal run, as you must have noticed. Brody and Elspeth had a rocky courtship. And that was nothing to Diarmid and Fiona's exploits, before they settled down to respectability and marital bliss. And if you look beyond my immediate family, Fergus and Marina are an unusual couple indeed, given she's pursued her artistic career with such success. By Jove, if I brought a simpering little miss home, straight out of the schoolroom and ignorant of anything but etiquette, I'd let the side down."

Tonight Kit had met the couples he'd mentioned. What had struck her about all of them was the contented air that clung about them. It was the same air she noticed with Hamish and Emily. It would be a dream come true, if she and Quentin could develop such trust and affection that strangers immediately saw the bond between them.

She reminded herself that it was early days yet, and she and her husband had made a good start. Perhaps in time, he could come to love her. He was already fond of her. His every action betrayed care and respect. And after last night, it was clear that they shared a mutual desire that she hoped might reinforce the link between them.

"What are you thinking about?" he asked, regarding her with an arrested expression.

Heat tinged her cheeks. "Last night. And this morning." She paused. "And this afternoon."

He groaned and to her surprise stumbled. Quentin was a graceful dancer. How very interesting that mention of what they did in bed suddenly gave him two left feet. Interesting and gratifying. It seemed Kit had some power over him, too.

A satisfied smile curled her lips. Aye, she and Quentin made an excellent beginning to their marriage.

"Don't torment me," he said, his tone gruff. "If I don't keep you downstairs until at least midnight, Emily will never forgive me."

Kit surveyed the glamorous crowd adorning this beautiful room with its lush seasonal decorations. Her ears rang with sweet music from Edinburgh's best dance orchestra. "I've never been to a ball before."

"It would be a pity to drag you away early then, even if I'm nearly mad with wanting you."

As she met his brilliant eyes, the breath caught in her throat. "I wish you could."

"Perhaps I can sneak you into a side room and kiss you."

That was an appealing idea. "As an early birthday present."

"But let's not hang about once midnight comes. It's torture not being able to touch you as I long to do."

Her smile faded. He didn't sound like he was joking. "I want to be alone with you, too, Quentin. This has been lovely, but nothing compares to what we do together."

He groaned again, and his grip on her waist firmed. "If this infernal waltz ever comes to an end, I'll sweep you away for a few kisses. Then we only have to last an hour or so to preserve appearances."

Her heart was racing, and not just from the energetic dancing. His hunger for her was exciting and flattering. "Emily and Hamish have been so good to us, we should stay a little longer."

He looked pained. "I'm beginning to feel like I married the etiquette lady."

"Do you mind?"

"No." A sly smile lifted his lips. "Because I've discovered that in private, you can be delightfully naughty."

She laughed, then laughed again with sheer happiness as he twirled her around the floor until she was breathless

Kit was lost in such a haze of private bliss that she didn't notice when the dancers around them slowed and faltered to a standstill. She only realized something untoward happened when the orchestra faded to silence.

"I seek my stepsister Christabel Urquhart, the Countess of Appin."

The haughty male voice rang out over the troubled whispers and turned her blood to ice. Kit shrank into Quentin's body and glanced around the room in instinctive panic. Surely there was some way to escape.

"Kit..." Quentin caught her hand, as the crowd parted to reveal Neil standing in the doorway on the other side of the huge room. Beside him stood the horrid Belmont Sinclair, Earl of Bogle. Half a dozen other men she didn't know ranged at her stepbrother's side. All were large and brawny and presented a silent promise of violence with their swords and heavy daggers. One or two were even armed with pistols.

God help her, someone in the glen must have talked. And Neil must have been close enough to finding her that he'd been in a position to listen, curse him.

"Let me go," she muttered, trying to break away from Quentin, her galloping heart threatening to burst out of her chest.

"Kit, there's nowhere to run," Quentin said, firming his grip. "We'll keep you safe."

She was so frantic, she hardly heard what he said. Her attention was all on her tormenter. As though he owned the house, Neil strode through the crowd in her direction. He definitely acted as though he owned her.

Feeling like a mouse in front of a snake, she cringed away. The buzz of curiosity around them rose then dropped to expectant silence when Neil spoke again. "Dear Christabel, we've all been so worried about you. How could you put us to such trouble? It's a silly prank that went too far, but now it's time to take you home to the people who love you."

Dazed and unmoving, Kit stared at Neil. The word love seemed a blasphemy on his lips. The only things Neil loved were himself and the Appin money. Money that for some reason he felt entitled to claim.

Despair weighted her stomach and made her mouth taste sour. Quentin was right. There was nowhere to run. The time for running had passed when Quentin had uncovered her secrets. After that, her avenues of escape had narrowed by the minute.

As Kit the stableboy, she might have a chance of getting away. But here in Lyon House and dressed as the countess she was, there was no way to evade her stepbrother.

Her view of the room retreated in an alarming manner. As she swayed, she felt a powerful arm curl around her waist. "By what right do you enter this house, you bastard?" Quentin asked, hauling Kit into his side. "Get the hell out."

Hamish strode up, bristling with anger. "I'm the Laird of Glen Lyon, and I'd like to know what the devil you think you're doing, bursting in on our Christmas revels without so much as a by-your-leave or an introduction."

Not shifting his gaze from Kit, Neil performed a perfunctory bow. "I'm Neil Maxwell of Halfrew, this lady's legal guardian. Under the law, you must return her to my custody."

"Like hell I will," Hamish snarled, standing large and belligerent on Kit's other side.

Neil's gaze didn't waver from Kit's face. "The game's up, Christabel. Belmont is here to marry you and take you back to Appin where you belong."

"Stop talking such confounded rubbish," Hamish snapped.

Quentin's nearness and Hamish's defense bolstered Kit's dwindling courage, although she shuddered to hear how reasonable Neil sounded. She struggled to summon her defiance, even as the memory of his domination made her tremble.

"I'm...I'm not going to marry Belmont."

Most of the guests had drawn back from the confrontation to watch what happened. How Kit wished that the room was full of the Douglas clan, as it had been last night at the ceilidh. A dozen stalwart stablehands wouldn't stand for her stepbrother's arrogance.

"Poor girl. You haven't been well." Neil's sham pity chilled her to the marrow. "Everyone knows you're delicate."

"Delicate? She's the bravest lassie I know," Hamish said, his size dwarfing Neil and his thugs. Kit could sense how much he wanted to pick her stepbrother up by the scruff of the neck and toss him out of Lyon House, but the intruders were heavily armed and nobody else in the ballroom was.

"Christabel, for everyone's sake, come quietly," Belmont said, reaching out for her. "The scandal will already be bad enough."

She flinched away from his touch. "Get away from me, you avaricious worm."

"That's my girl," Quentin said.

His approval reminded her that she was no longer friendless and at Neil's mercy. At last – too late in her opinion – she straightened her backbone and lifted her chin to face Neil down.

Her unthinking terror receded, as she sucked in a breath that cleared her swimming head. She had Quentin and the people of Glen Lyon on her side. Neil had bullied her for years, but he'd never bully her again, damn him.

"I'm not coming with you, Neil," she said in a firm voice. "So go back to Appin and pack your belongings and get off my lands."

"I can see all this has been too much for you." Neil responded with more of that unconvincing sympathy. "It's no surprise. Your wits have always been feeble."

Kit's temper stirred, vanquishing the last of her weakness, and she glared at this man who had tormented her for too long. "When I turn twenty-one, I take control of my inheritance."

"Not if you're of unsound mind, and I've got half a dozen men with me, ready to swear to your imbecility." Neil's superior expression was lamentably familiar. He still thought he could win, even now. "This mad act of running away to become a stablehand speaks to the frailty of your nerves. Once I set out the sad facts, no judge in the land will give you control of the Appin estates."

In the face of his self-assurance, her confidence faltered. Kit's frightened gaze swept the crowded room. Could anyone here be ready to believe Neil's lies? The problem was that her stepbrother sounded so plausible. The toad always sounded so plausible.

"I'm not mad," she said, detesting how her voice trembled. "You should rather look to your own future. Once I lay what you've done at Appin before the courts, you'll be lucky to escape prison."

"So sad to see you like this." Neil's expression conveyed insincere regret. "Completely insane."

"Prove it," Quentin snapped.

"I've got the minister from Appin outside." Neil didn't spare Quentin a glance. "He's ready to perform the marriage ceremony for Christabel and Lord Bogle. He, too, will swear the girl hasn't been in her fit mind since she was a child."

"Yet this paragon is willing to marry this pathetic creature to your friend?" Hamish asked sarcastically, stepping closer to Neil and further away from Kit. She missed his brawny presence at her side.

"Belmont is the right man to care for her in her distress."

Kit chanced a glance around the room and met a wall of avid eyes, but she was too upset to read what impact Neil's story had on the onlookers. There was one consolation. Whatever the outcome of tonight's intrusion, at least she was safe from ever having to marry Belmont.

"You're too late, Neil," Kit said with satisfaction. "I'm already married. Under the terms of the will, once I wed, I gain control of my fortune."

Shock leached the color from her stepbrother's face, then a flash of such coruscating anger blazed in his eyes that she cowered against Quentin.

"You little bitch, you'd do anything to spite me." Neil spoke over the onlookers' audible gasps of horror. "Given the doubts over your sanity, I'll have any match overturned."

"No, you will not," Quentin insisted, stepping in front of Kit. "Christabel is my wife, and you'll take her from me over my dead body."

Neil wrenched the sword from the scabbard at his hip. "That can be arranged, whoever in Hades you are."

A few of the ladies shrieked, as the guests retreated further toward the walls. With impressive speed, Neil's cohorts drew their own weapons and created a tight circle around Kit and Quentin. Kit surveyed the pitiless faces observing her, and her fear stirred anew.

"Dinnae be a fool, man," Fergus Mackinnon said, moving up beside Hamish. "It's clear you've lost. Murder and mayhem willnae change that."

"By God, I'm not beaten yet," Neil growled. He lurched forward to grab Kit, but Quentin kept her out of reach.

"Quentin, here!"

Through a mist of rising panic, Kit saw Diarmid wrench a ceremonial sword from a display on the wall and toss it across to her husband. More cries of shock from the crowd, and at last a few of the gentlemen advanced with a hint of aggression.

"Much obliged, cuz!" Quentin caught the sword in one hand with a deftness and confidence that did wonders to revive her spirits. "Drop your weapon, Maxwell. Even with your men, you can't hope to prevail against a crowd of this size."

As Neil edged around, seeking an opening, Diarmid marched around the room and passed swords to some of the other men, including Fergus and Hamish and Brody.

"Neil, it might be sensible to make a strategic retreat," Belmont bleated, inching away and eyeing the forces that assembled against them. Kit noticed that while her suitor was armed, he hadn't yet unsheathed his weapon. "The gamble hasn't paid off."

"Be buggered if I'm going to fail at this late stage," Neil blustered.

"You'll have to kill me to take me away from here," Kit said with a calmness that in no way reflected the frenzied pounding of her heart. "And if I'm dead, the estate goes to cousin Stephen."

"You've lost, Maxwell," Quentin said, raising the sword. His face was set in determined lines, and his jaw was square with purpose. "My wife has the victory."

At last Neil seemed to realize the danger he was in. He swung his head from side to side like a trapped rat. In the fraught silence that descended, the clock in the hall began to strike midnight.

CHAPTER FOURTEEN

he Maxwell bastard was good-looking.

Quentin hadn't expected that, for some reason. Now he stared into that highbred, saturnine face and felt a pang of irrational jealousy.

And fear.

After last night's astonishing mixture of passion and tenderness, the idea of living without his Christmas countess was unbearable. He and his lovely bride had years of happiness ahead of them – and he wasn't letting this mongrel get in the way of that.

"That's the clock marking the start of Christmas Day," Kit said in a steady voice. Quentin's heart leaped at her extraordinary courage. "I'm twenty-one. Even if I wasn't already married, you'd have lost, Neil."

"What time were you born?" Neil asked, desperate to claw back a few hours to change the inevitable outcome.

"What can it matter now?" Hamish growled.

To Quentin's surprise, Kit smiled. "Five minutes past midnight. I've managed to stay out of your greedy clutches just long enough. And you must know you'll never prove me mad. I've got a whole clan of Urquharts willing to swear to your depredations on the estate and your cruel treatment of me."

Quentin's chest expanded with pride, as he heard her steady defiance of this man who had bullied her for so long. "Not to mention everyone here on the Glen Lyon estate."

Neil was looking haggard. He must know this last gambit had failed, but he wasn't yet ready to admit defeat.

"I can still kill the swine you married." Another scandalized mutter rose from the watching crowd as Neil raised his sword, but Quentin was close enough to see that most of the fight had gone out of him.

"You can try," he said evenly, his hand tightening on the old-fashioned sword's basket hilt.

To his surprise, he found an unlikely supporter in the blond Adonis at Neil's side, who while pretty, was clearly nowhere near as powerful a character. "By God, I've had enough of this. You'll hang if you kill anyone, and it's more than likely I'll hang with you. To hell with that idea, Neil. Let the snotty little cow go. I don't fancy a wife who's been hanging around in the stables for the last month, even if she comes gold-plated. The devil knows what she's been up to since she left Appin. She's probably spread her legs for every lout she's met on her travels."

An appalled hum rippled through the crowd, as Quentin leveled his sword at the man's throat. "You will apologize for that, or I'll kill you where you stand."

Neil might have braved it out, but Lord Bogle wasn't made of such stout stuff. He went pasty white, gulped for air, and spread his leather-gloved hands in surrender. "Sorry, old man. Sour grapes for losing out. Didn't know what I was saying. Your pardon, my lady."

Neil surveyed the room with wild eyes, but he must have realized that even with six bully boys to support him, he couldn't prevail. With a furious hiss, he lowered his sword and shoved it back in its scabbard. "You're welcome to the damned termagant. Any man who takes on Christabel Urquhart is destined to live in misery."

"And I was always so terrifically fond of you, Neil," Kit said with poisonous sweetness.

"Get out," Quentin said implacably, even now holding his blade at the ready. He didn't yet trust Neil to make the sensible choice and leave.

Hamish and Fergus stepped up to seize Neil's arms, just in case he decided to make some last act of defiance, but by now, Quentin read acceptance of failure in the man's expression.

"I should lock you up for disturbing the peace," Hamish said grimly.

At last, Quentin lowered his sword and held his hand out toward Kit. With a choked sob, she dived straight for him. She wrapped her arms tight around him and buried her head in his chest.

He twined his arm around her and kissed the top of her ruffled dark head. Relief flooded him in such a powerful tide that his head reeled.

They'd won. By all that was holy, they'd won.

"It's over, sweetheart." As he looked around the room, he read a similar relief on every face that the confrontation ended without bloodshed. And with Kit safe and where she belonged. "You don't have to be frightened anymore."

When Kit turned in Quentin's hold, he didn't let her go. After the terror that had gripped him when he feared Neil might prevail, he couldn't bear to have her out of reach.

"Just throw them out, please, Hamish," she said, her voice unsteady. "The scandal is going to be bad enough anyway, without bringing the law into it. And I don't want anyone here to get hurt."

His arm remaining around Kit, Quentin watched as Hamish and Fergus marched Neil across the ballroom. Her odious stepbrother tripped and cried out as Hamish hauled him roughly across the floor. Then Quentin and Kit joined the other guests, who flooded into the hall to watch Neil ejected from Lyon House. Neil stumbled down the flight of stone steps and landed on his knees in the snow.

"And don't come back," Hamish said, as Neil's cohorts rushed out after their leader.

"You have no right..." Neil protested, struggling to his feet with Bogle's aid, before one of the ruffians decided to try and help as well. The man slipped on the icy surface and all three went down in a jumble of legs. The air turned blue with cursing.

Jeering laughter rang out from the audience who observed events through the huge windows. Quentin wasn't surprised to note that Neil looked livid as he staggered to his feet. It was no news that Kit's stepbrother suffered from overweening pride. His self-importance would never recover from tonight's comprehensive defeat, and now his undignified exit from Lyon House. In the space of a few minutes, the bastard had changed from a menace to a clown.

Good.

Quentin joined Hamish on the wide front steps and spoke in a ringing voice. "My wife and I intend to travel to Appin in the next few days. You will be gone from the property by then – and don't think to ransack the place in the meantime. If you do, scandal be damned. I'll prosecute you to the full measure of the law."

"I deserve better than this," Neil spluttered, as another of his men hoisted him to his feet with more success than the last attempt. "I've devoted myself to the Appin estate."

"Devoted yourself to feathering your own nest, more like," Kit said, her voice colder than the freezing air as she stepped up beside Quentin. "You've been fiddling the accounts for years. Nothing you've done has been a secret. You always forgot that the people of Appin owe their loyalty to me and not to you. There's ample evidence to have you up on trial. So don't try and help yourself to anything extra before you go. You've stolen more than enough from me over the years. If you've any sense, you'll go back to your lands and stay there."

"Bravo, my bonny," Quentin murmured, taking her hand in his.

Until now, he'd seen Kit in many guises, from stableboy to irresistible lover. But at this moment, with a touch of awe, he recognized the centuries of command that ran through her bloodline. She was truly the Countess of Appin at last.

"Curse you. Curse every one of you. And curse that slut, the Countess of Appin. May she rot in hell," Neil bit out.

Quentin surged forward to give the brute the thrashing he deserved, but Kit caught his arm. "No, let him go. He's angry because we've triumphed."

"It would give me immense satisfaction to knock the teeth down his throat, then kick his filthy rump back to the Borders."

"I'm sure. But I'd much rather you stayed here with me."

She had a point, he supposed. He watched Neil limp away, trailed by his henchmen. Further down the drive Quentin could make out the shadowy forms of the horses that the unwelcome visitors must have ridden up to Lyon House. Neil and his cohorts would have an uncomfortable journey to wherever they managed to find shelter now. He hoped they froze their bloody arses off.

Emily appeared at Kit's side. "Are you all right, Kit?"

Kit turned to her with a relieved smile. "I feel like I've reached the end of a nightmare. It's thanks to you and Hamish and Quentin that I've managed to come through."

With the physical ease that always made Quentin envious, Hamish put his arm around his wife. How he hoped that one day he and Kit might share the same closeness. "We helped, Kit, but it was your courage and resourcefulness that won the day. I'm proud to have you in the family."

Quentin watched Kit's expression change. For the first time, he saw her free of fear. She'd been lovely before. In the light reflected from the open doors behind her, his bride was so beautiful, she stole his breath away.

"I'm privileged to call you my kin," she said in a voice thick with emotion.

"Och, and now it's Christmas Day and time to celebrate," Fergus said from behind Hamish. The tall red-headed man had his arms around his gorgeous wife Marina.

Quentin turned to Kit. "Not just Christmas, but Kit's birthday, too. Happy birthday, my lovely wife."

As Kit stared up at him, the radiance in her eyes made his heart swell. "Thank you, Quentin. For the first time in years, it really is going to be a happy birthday. I've come into my inheritance. Appin will soon be free of the Maxwells. And I've just married the most wonderful man in the world."

"Oh, Kit..." Ignoring their audience, he swept her up for a passionate kiss. By the time he raised his head, they were both gasping. "Now let's get inside before you turn into an icicle. You and I have some dancing to do."

CHAPTER FIFTEEN

It was after two before Kit and Quentin managed to slip away from the ball. Everyone present was so eager to congratulate her on defeating Neil and wish her a happy birthday. Everyone wanted to hear more of her adventures.

She wasn't optimistic enough to imagine that the wider world would offer such unqualified approval, once the story of the stableboy countess leaked out, as it inevitably would. But to the people at Glen Lyon tonight, she was a heroine.

All the time, Quentin remained at her side with his arm around her waist, smiling at her as if she was the most glorious creature he'd ever beheld. Every time she looked into his brilliant hazel eyes, a shiver of excitement rippled through her. Because while it was lovely to be welcomed into Hamish and Emily's circle with such enthusiasm, she'd spent last night exploring a new and dazzling world. As time went on, she ached to be alone with her husband and have his hands on her, without several hundred pairs of eyes observing them.

Constant physical contact heated the blood in her veins. So she was trembling when they finally managed to break free and climb the stairs to their rooms.

"You were so brave when Neil threatened you," she said, tightening her grip on his hand. "I was afraid he really was going to kill you."

"Och, there were a hundred brawny Highlanders in that room ready to come to my defense if that weasel tried anything."

That wasn't how she remembered it. When Neil had brandished his sword before Quentin, alarm had clawed a rift across her heart. She knew her stepbrother's temper well enough to recognize that facing defeat, he could well have chosen the reckless option.

As they turned down the corridor, Quentin went on. "You're braver by far than I ever was. You've had to be brave for years. I honor you, Christabel."

He stopped outside their room, but instead of pushing the door open, he drew her into his arms for a lingering kiss that left her shaking.

"I can hardly believe I'm free," she murmured, staring up into Quentin's eyes and reading a steadfast affection there that she prayed would one day turn to love.

So many of her hopes had come to fruition tonight. Was it greedy to ask for one more miracle?

Quentin's smile faded, and his expression turned serious. "Except you're married to me, when you were so close to making it on your own."

A tender smile curved her lips, as she laid her hand on his cheek. He'd shaved before the ball, but that was hours ago now. Whiskers prickled against her palm. She found these physical details of the man she loved endlessly fascinating. Like all young girls, she'd dreamed of the gentleman she'd marry. But those dreams had been insipid, compared to her husband's vital reality.

"I've been on my own too much. Now I have a family. Now I have a gallant laddie to call husband. Now I have a chance to create a family of my own. This has been the most perfect Christmas I've ever known. Despite Neil doing his best to spoil it." Her tone turned gloating. "Although watching Hamish toss him out into the snow was a nice moment."

Quentin's eyes lit, and he placed his hand over hers. "By God, I love you, Kit. You're a braw wife for a Highlander."

All the breath whooshed out of her lungs. Shocked, she stared at him. "What...what did you say?"

He kept hold of her hand. "You're a braw wife."

Was she dreaming indeed? "Not that bit," she stammered.

He frowned. "The part about loving you?"

"Aye. That part."

He glanced down the empty corridor and finally pushed the door open. "I think we need privacy for this discussion."

Speechless with rising hope – when for so many years hope had been a stranger – she let Quentin lead her inside. He released her hand to close the door as she stopped in the center of the room.

She watched him bend his head as if gathering his thoughts – or saying a silent prayer. Her heart raced like the Derby winner she dreamed of breeding and every muscle in her body was taut, while she waited to hear again the words she longed for. Surely she couldn't have mistaken him, but she'd been afraid so long, she needed to be sure.

Slowly he turned to face her. There was no trace of charming, humorous Quentin MacNab in his face.

He looked somber, and older than she'd ever seen him. "The first time I saw you, I reacted in a way I've never before reacted to a stableboy. I realized almost immediately that you were a girl – and a bonny one at that. So I watched you. I watched you a lot. I learned a great deal about you from close observation, despite your best efforts to stay out of my way."

She made a helpless gesture. "I feared that you might guess I wasn't what I pretended to be. I feared that you might notice that I was...watching you, too."

"I did notice. I hoped one day that you'd trust me enough to tell me your story and let me help you."

"A snowy night granted your wish."

He didn't exactly smile, but his austere expression eased a fraction. "Aye. A snowy night, where interest and admiration and the itch of physical attraction tumbled over into something much more momentous. Tumbled over into...love."

The word shuddered through her like a blow, although she'd been preparing to hear it again since he'd launched his explanation. She stayed quiet as he went on. "Then I faced a dilemma. In your short life, you'd already been compelled to so much. I'd already decided to court you, once you were free of Neil and able to make a choice of your own volition. But because we'd been alone together overnight, you were compelled yet again, this time to marry me. I hated that, even if it meant my dearest wishes coming true."

She swallowed to shift the jagged lump of emotion blocking her throat. Then swallowed again. "I wanted to marry you, too."

It was as if he didn't hear her. He went on in that low, grave, very un-Quentin-like voice. "Yet instead of offering me a grudging acceptance, you welcomed me as your husband with such generosity and passion last night that I fell in love with you all over again. Now I'm so deep in love with you, I'm never going to surface again."

His voice turned husky with emotion. "Kit, tell me I have a chance. Tell me that one day you might love me as I love you. Tell me that I can live with hope. Because I die of love for you, my beautiful wife."

She blinked back tears, and her legs trembled beneath her. Her heart expanded until it felt ready to burst out of her chest. "Quentin…"

"Can you love me, Kit?"

She raised shaking hands to dash the tears from her eyes, and a tremulous smile lifted her lips. "I can. I will." She stepped toward him. It seemed obscene that she wasn't in his arms right now. "I do. Always."

He studied her, as if he needed to winnow her words before he could trust them. "You…love me?"

A choked giggle escaped, and she spread her hands. "I love you, Quentin. I loved you even before you coaxed me into that hut and ruined my reputation."

Relief filled her, as a smile set appealing creases around his eyes. "Well, that's all right, then."

She stepped closer, until she was only a foot away from him. "I think…I think this is the moment you should kiss me."

An arrested expression passed across his face. That dear, quirky, beautiful face that had filled her dreams for so many weeks. Since she'd first seen him. The face that would watch over her for the rest of their lives together.

"You know, you may have that right, my lovely countess."

With breathtaking power, he drew her into his arms and pressed his lips to hers in a declaration of love victorious. Kit kissed him back with all the adoration in her heart and a silent promise for a golden future stretching ahead of them.

She'd come through. She'd won. Now the world offered her an unrivaled gift of love and hope.

It was her birthday. It was Christmas. It was a happy ending for her personal fairy tale.

She was the luckiest girl in Scotland.

EPILOGUE

Glen Lyon House, Christmas Eve, 1835

Christabel MacNab, Countess of Appin, hooked her gloved hand around her dashing husband's elbow and smiled with pleasure as she surveyed the crowded ballroom spread out before her. Winter greenery decorated the room and added a fresh scent to the air. Edinburgh's best dance orchestra played the latest waltz, and sparkling chandeliers cast golden enchantment across the cheerful throng.

Quentin looked spectacular in his Highlander garb, an inevitable reminder of that fateful Christmas ball five years ago, when she'd shaken off Neil Maxwell's baleful influence and even better, she'd discovered that her marriage was a love match after all. Since then, she and Quentin had established a good and purposeful life at a thriving Appin. A life so busy that this was her first Christmas trip to Glen Lyon since her wedding, although there had been plenty of visits at other times. Hamish and Emily and their children were family, and time had only strengthened the immediate affinity she'd felt with the Douglases.

"Kit, *bella*, how wonderful to see you here!" Marina, Lady of Achnasheen, exclaimed in her exuberant way, as she rushed up on the arm of her imposing husband, Fergus Mackinnon. A flurry of embraces ensued. "That color is *perfetto* on you."

"Thank you," Kit said. The rose pink gown was one of her favorites, and she was delighted that her hair had grown enough for the elaborately curled hairstyles now in vogue. The countess crop had enjoyed a brief popularity after her wedding, but longer hair had become the mode. "You look as beautiful as ever."

"It's been much too long since we've seen you, *per pietà*," Marina went on.

Fergus laughed down at the dark-eyed, half-Italian beauty. "Do ye no' recall that we visited Appin in October, *mo chridhe?*"

Marina flashed him a brilliant smile. "It feels like a long time. I want to paint a portrait of the *piccolo* Connor while he's still a toddler."

"You'll have to catch him first," Quentin said drily, a wealth of love for his mischievous son warming his wry humor.

"And he's fiendishly fast." Kit's hands came to rest on her rounded stomach. She was expecting another baby in March. "I haven't a chance of keeping up with him these days."

"Perhaps ye should enter him in the Derby," Fergus said with a laugh, putting his arm around his wife.

"Wait until you see my new colt, and you'll regret mocking my ambitions," Kit retorted.

So far, her dream of breeding a champion hadn't eventuated. Neil had run the once-famous Appin stables down so badly that it had taken years of work to bring them back to standard. But under Laing's supervision, this last crop of foals showed definite promise, and one particular bay had the fire in his heart and the strength and speed to encourage her hopes.

"Are ye sharing racing tips, Kit?" Diarmid had been waltzing with his pretty blond wife Fiona, but now they stopped to join the conversation. "Och, I won a fortune on that outsider ye recommended last September."

Quentin snickered at her side. "My wife made excellent use of her time as a stableboy."

"Nothing like a bit of practical experience to back up all my reading," Kit said pertly.

"Well, dinnae waste any inside knowledge on Fergus here," Diarmid said, digging his childhood friend in the ribs. "He's already far too rich for his own good."

Fergus laughed again, as Fiona shook her head in sham disappointment. "It's Christmas, my love. Can't you laddies be nice to one another just once a year?"

"Fergus would think we were sick if we were nice to him," Hamish said in his bass rumble from just behind Kit. "He'd sit down in a gloomy corner and fret himself into a decline."

"Yes, that's true," Emily said with a laugh. Looking magnificent in a spangled silk dress that displayed her lush bosom to advantage, she held her husband's hand. "They turn into a bunch of schoolboys when they get together. That will never change."

"You're lucky you married a sensible man, my love," Quentin said. His green-gold glance worked the same devastating effect on her pulses as it had all those years ago, when she was desperate to hide her penchant for the laird's spectacular nephew.

She arched supercilious eyebrows. "Oh, and is that what I did?"

Although he was right. The gossip out in the wider world had been awful, once the story of her disguise and rushed marriage broke. During their early years together, there had been many occasions when she'd appreciated Quentin's steady temperament and steadfast love. Luckily the worst of the tattle had faded over time. And of course, the people they loved, most of whom were here tonight, had never given a fig for the nasty talk.

"Aye, had you forgotten?" He leaned forward and kissed her in a way that nobody would ever describe as sensible.

By the time he raised his head, her knees were buckling. That hadn't changed either.

She drifted back to the real world to hear Hamish and Diarmid discussing Neil Maxwell's recent misfortunes. "Did ye hear he was tossed out of the Tories for graft and corruption? I'd say his political career isnae going anywhere," Diarmid was saying.

Once the mere mention of Neil's name would have been enough to set Kit trembling, but these days, the Countess of Appin and her dashing husband had nothing to fear from her cur of a stepbrother. She held so much evidence of his thefts at Appin that Neil knew coming within a hundred miles of her was asking for trouble.

"Neil bloody Maxwell is the last person we need in government," Hamish snorted.

"Don't spoil our Christmas party with talk of that horrid man," Emily said. "Especially as this is our chance to enjoy ourselves free of parental duties. Tomorrow we'll do nothing but keep our children out of mischief. You know what they're like when they're all together."

"Aye, I do," Hamish said with a longsuffering sigh, although the spark in his eye hinted that he intended to encourage any high spirits that might be afoot.

Kit smiled, as she recalled Connor's glee at having a whole week at Glen Lyon with his cousins and the other children. There were at least twenty bairns sleeping upstairs in the nurseries right now – although she had her doubts if much actual sleeping was taking place.

Apart from Connor, there were Fergus and Marina's three, Hamish and Emily's two, Brody and Elspeth's four, and Diarmid and Fiona's five. Not to mention assorted extras. Christmas tomorrow promised to be joyous chaos. She could hardly wait.

"In that case, there's no time to lose." Quentin smiled down at her with the unabashed admiration that never ceased to make her want to melt into a puddle of warm syrup. "May I have this dance, Christabel?"

"I'd love that," she said, accepting his hand. "Although I can't promise that I'll be too light on my feet."

"You're always the soul of grace to me, my darling."

His gentle teasing made her giggle. Connor had been a large baby, and she'd felt like a whale by the time her tawny-headed son had emerged squalling into the world. "Just keep thinking that."

"You'll be beautiful to me as long as I live, sweetheart." Quentin's arm curled around her waist, and he swept her out into the whirling dancers. "I love you, my favorite stableboy."

Her eternally susceptible heart did one of its now familiar flips. She never tired of hearing him declare his love. Which was a good thing, because he did it with delightful frequency.

"And I love you with all my being, my wonderful husband." She trailed her hand up his shoulder to tangle her fingers in the silky hair at his nape. It was a silent promise of many more caresses to come. "You were the best Christmas present ever."

ABOUT THE AUTHOR

Australian Anna Campbell has written 11 multi award-winning historical romances for Avon HarperCollins and Grand Central Publishing. As an independently published author, she's released more than 30 bestselling stories. Right now, she is working on a new series called A Scandal in Mayfair, set amidst the glamour and sensuality of Regency London. Anna has won numerous awards for her stories, including RT Book Reviews Reviewers Choice, the Booksellers Best, the Golden Quill (three times), the Heart of Excellence (twice), the Write Touch, the Aspen Gold (twice), and the Australian Romance Readers' favorite historical romance (five times).

Anna loves to hear from her readers. You can find her at:

Website: www.annacampbell.com

facebook.com/AnnaCampbellFans

twitter.comAnnaCampbellOz

bookbub.com/authors/anna-campbell

The Laird's Willful Lass:
The Lairds Most Likely Book 1

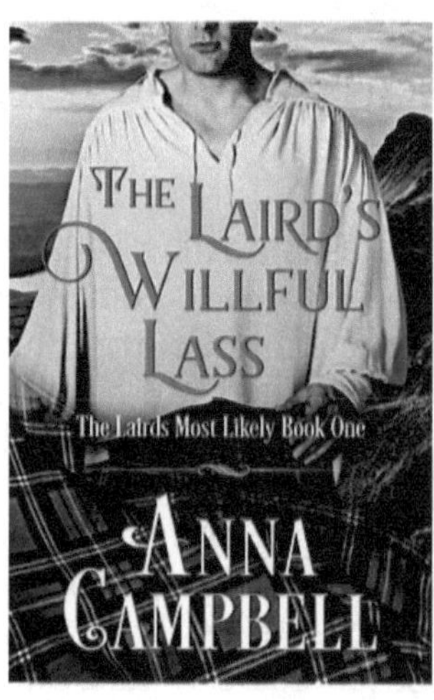

***An untamed man as immovable as a
Highland mountain...***

Fergus Mackinnon, autocratic Laird of Achnasheen,
likes to be in charge. When he was little more than
a lad, he became master of his Scottish estate, and
he's learned to rely on his unfailing judgment. So
has everyone else in his corner of the world. He sees
no reason for his bride—when he finds her—to be
any different.

***A headstrong woman from the warm and
passionate south...***

Marina Lucchetti knows all about fighting her way
through a wall of masculine arrogance. In her
native Florence, she's become a successful artist, no
easy feat for a woman. Now a commission to paint a
series of Highland scenes promises to spread her

fame far and wide. When a carriage accident strands her at Achnasheen for a few weeks, it's a mixed blessing. The magnificent landscape offers everything her artistic soul could desire. If only she can resist the impulse to smash her easel across the laird's obstinate head.

When two fiery souls come together, a conflagration flares.

Marina is Fergus's worst nightmare—a woman who defies a man's guidance. Fergus challenges everything Marina believes about a woman's right to choose her path. No two people could be less suited. But when irresistible passion enters the equation, good sense soon jumps into the loch.

Will the desire between Fergus and Marina blaze hot, then fade to ashes? Or will the imperious laird and his willful lass discover that their differences aren't insurmountable after all, but the spice that will flavor a lifetime of happiness?

The Laird's Christmas Kiss:
The Lairds Most Likely Book 2

Down with love!

Ever since she was fifteen, shy wallflower Elspeth
Douglas has pined in vain for the attentions of
dashing Brody Girvan, Laird of Invermackie. But
the rakish Highlander doesn't even know she's
alive. Now she's twenty, she realizes that she'll
never be happy until she stops loving her brother's
handsome friend. When family and friends gather
at Achnasheen Castle for Christmas, she intends to
show the world that she's all grown up, and grown
out of silly crushes on gorgeous Scotsmen. So take
that, my gallant laddie!

Girls just want to have fun...

Except it turns out that Brody isn't singing from the
same Christmas carol sheet. Elspeth decides she's

not interested in him anymore, just as he decides
he's very interested indeed. In fact, now he looks
more closely, his friend Hamish's sister is pretty
and funny and forthright – and just the lassie to
share his Highland estate. Convincing his little
wren of his romantic intentions is difficult enough,
even before she undergoes a makeover and
becomes the belle of Achnasheen. For once in his
life, dissolute Brody is burdened with honorable
intentions, while the lady he pursues is set on
flirtation with no strings attached.

Deck the halls with mistletoe!

With interfering friends and a crate of imported
mistletoe thrown into the mix, the stage is set for a
house party rife with secrets, clandestine kisses,
misunderstandings, heartache, scandal, and love
triumphant.

The Highlander's Lost Lady:
The Lairds Most Likely Book 3

A Highlander as brave and strong as a knight of old...

When Diarmid Mactavish, Laird of Invertavey, discovers a mysterious woman washed up on his land after a wild storm, he takes her in and tries to find her family. But even as forbidden dreams of sensual fulfillment torment him, he's convinced that this beautiful lassie isn't what she seems. And if there's one thing Diarmid despises, it's a liar.

A mother willing to do anything to save her daughter...

Widow Fiona Grant has risked everything to break free of her clan and rescue her adolescent daughter from a forced marriage. But before her quest has barely begun, disaster strikes. She escapes her brutish kinsmen, only to be shipwrecked on Mactavish territory where she falls into her enemies' hands. For centuries, a murderous feud has raged between the Mactavishes and the Grants, so how can she trust her darkly handsome host?

Now a twisted Highland road leads to danger and passion...and irresistible love. But is love strong enough to banish the past's long shadows and offer these wary allies all that their hearts desire?

The Highlander's Defiant Captive:
The Lairds Most Likely Book 4

Peace in the glens means war in the bedchamber!

Scotland. 1699. In a time of heroes, the greatest hero of all is Callum Mackinnon, Laird of Achnasheen. Brave, reckless, canny, and handsome enough to turn any lassie weak at the knees, Callum is a legend in the wild corner of the Highlands where he rules. Now the young laird is determined to choose a new path for his clan and end the violent feud with the Drummonds, a conflict that has painted the glens red with blood for centuries. This means taking Bonny Mhairi Drummond, the Rose of Bruard, as his wife. When negotiations with her pig-headed father break down, Callum seizes matters into his own hands and kidnaps the fairest maiden in Scotland, swearing to make her his own.

Bonny Mhairi is the adored only child of Clan

Drummond's doughty chieftain and she's inherited all her father's courage and stubbornness. Not to mention his undying hatred for anyone called Mackinnon. When the Mackinnon chieftain steals her away from her home and vows to woo her into accepting him as her husband, she swears that she'll never consent to be his bride. But trapped inside her foe's castle, Mhairi finds it hard to cling to old certainties. She detests her arrogant jailer, even as he sparks a fierce, forbidden hunger in her soul.

Loving the enemy...

As Callum and Mhairi wage their passionate war of hearts, danger, treachery and desire circle closer and closer. When her father's army masses at the gates of Achnasheen, will Mhairi prove herself a Drummond now and forever? Or will new allegiances trump ancient hatred, as the desperate laird battles to win the lass he loves more than his life?

The Highlander's Christmas Quest:
The Lairds Most Likely Book 5

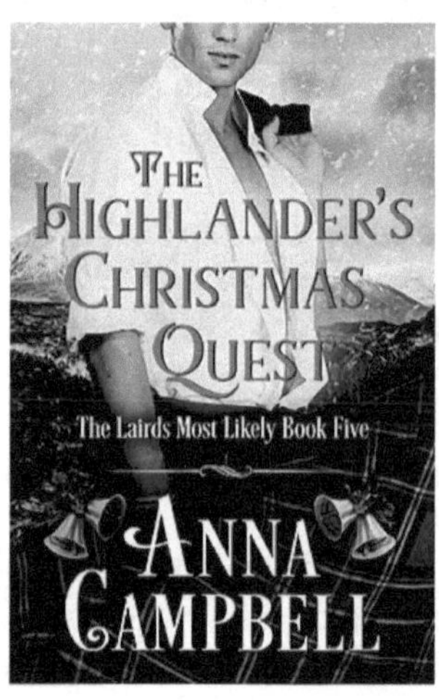

She's found the man for her, but he has no plans to stay on her island. Perhaps it's time to try a little sabotage!

Scotland. 1725. The moment she sees handsome Dougal Drummond, Kirsty Macbain tumbles headlong into love. A chance storm a few days before Christmas has blown the gallant Highlander off-course to her father's isle of Askaval, but once he's repaired his boat, Dougal is determined to continue on his way. His bright blue eyes are firmly fixed on valiant deeds and a distant horizon. What does he care for a smart-mouthed, independent lassie who forms no part of his plans for his future?

Kirsty is convinced that if only she can keep Dougal on Askaval, he'll see how perfect they are together. With his boat out of action, he's trapped in her company. Some surreptitious midnight destruction with a drill and a hammer might help true love to win out. On the other hand, if Dougal discovers what she's been up to, there will be the devil to pay.

Will this madcap Christmas deliver Kirsty's heart's desire – or will her scheming see Dougal sailing away to a life without her?

The Highlander's English Bride:
The Lairds Most Likely Book 6

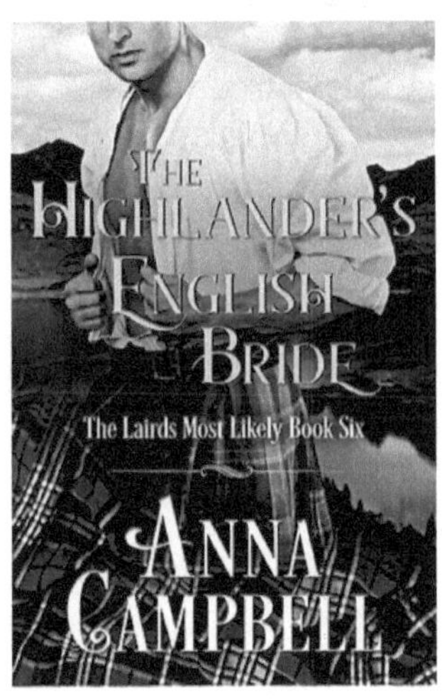

An impossible pairing...

Hamish Douglas, the mercurial Laird of Glen Lyon, has never got along with independent, smart-mouthed Emily Baylor. Which wouldn't matter if this brilliant Scottish astronomer didn't move in the same scientific circles as Emily and if her famous father wasn't his mentor. But when Emily looks likely to derail the event which will make Hamish's career, he loses his temper with the pretty miss and his recklessness leaves her reputation in ruins.

A marriage made in scandal...

Emily has always thought her father's spectacular protégé was far too arrogant for his own good. But what is she to do when the only way she can save her good name in society is to wed the unruly laird? Reluctantly she accepts Hamish's proposal, but only on the condition that their union remains chaste. That shouldn't be a problem; they've never been friends, let alone potential lovers – except that after they marry, Hamish reveals unexpected depths and a host of admirable qualities, and he's so awfully handsome, and now the swaggering rogue admits that he desires her...

From the ballrooms of London to the grandeur of the western Highlands, a battle royal rages between these two strong-willed combatants. Neither plans to yield an inch – but are these smart people smart enough to see that sometimes the greatest victory lies in mutual surrender?

The Highlander's Forbidden Mistress:
The Lairds Most Likely Book 7

A week to be wicked...

Widowed Selina Martin faces another marriage
founded on duty, not love. When notorious
libertine Lord Bruard invites her to his isolated
hunting lodge, he promises discretion – and seven
days of hedonistic pleasure before she weds her
boorish fiancé. All her life, Selina has done the right
thing, but this no-strings-attached chance to
discover the handsome rake's sensual secrets is
irresistible. She'll surrender to her wicked fantasies,
seize some brief happiness, then knuckle down to a
loveless union. What could possibly go wrong?

In a lifetime of seduction, Brock Drummond, the
dashing Earl of Bruard, has never wanted a woman
the way he wants demure widow Selina Martin.
When Selina agrees to become his temporary lover,
he soon falls captive to an enchantment unlike any

other. He sets out to slake his white hot desire until only ashes remain, but as each day of forbidden delight passes, the idea of saying goodbye to his ardent mistress becomes more and more unbearable.

When scandal explodes around them and threatens to destroy Selina, Brock is the only person she can turn to. After so short a time, can she trust a man whose name is a byword for depravity?

Will this sizzling liaison prove a mere affair to remember? Or will their week of passion spark a lifetime of happiness for the widow and her dissolute Scottish earl?

The Highlander's Christmas Countess: The Lairds Most Likely Book 8

The new stableboy has a secret!

Kit Laing is a genius with Glen Lyon's horses and a favorite with his employer's family, but he isn't all he seems. In fact, the shy stablehand isn't a he at all. Kit is actually Christabel Urquhart, Countess of Appin, on the run from a greedy, violent stepbrother with designs on her fortune.

And the laird's handsome nephew has worked out just what it is.

Quentin MacNab, the dashing heir to Cannich, has had his suspicions about the new stable lad from the first. Kit is far too pretty to be a boy – and far too well spoken to be a servant.

***Now passion and danger combine to create a Yuletide like no other.**most*

When a snowstorm traps Kit and Quentin overnight in an isolated hut, the discovery of her true identity sparks a rushed marriage to stave off a scandal. But can the Christmas Countess learn to trust her charming new husband's promises of protection? Or will their fragile alliance fall victim to the evil forces assailing her?

The Highlander's Rescued Maiden: The Lairds Most Likely Book 9

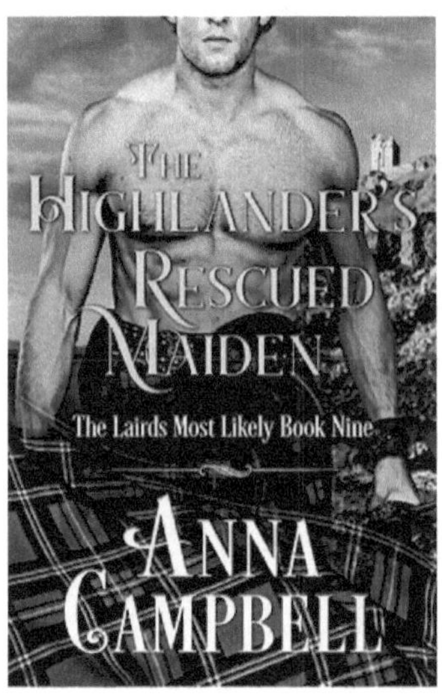

The myth of Fair Ellen of the Isles.

Across the Highlands, people recount the legend of a beautiful lassie in a tower, locked away from her clamorous suitors by a tyrannical father. Any person of sense dismisses the story as a fairy tale, no more substantial than a wisp of Scottish mist.

Rogue or hero? Or a little bit of both?

Dashing Highlander Will Mackinnon is a devil with the ladies, disinclined to fall for such romantic nonsense. But one day, his storm-tossed boat washes ashore at a rocky island dominated by a stone tower. Inside the tower, he discovers lovely, gallant Ellen Cameron and a passion that eclipses anything he's experienced before in his reckless life.

Danger and desire...

This brave adventurer vows to rescue the captive maiden and make her his own forever. But dark shadows gather about the lovers and threaten to destroy all their hopes for happiness. Will has found the love of a lifetime – but will it end up costing him his life?

The Highlander's Christmas Lassie:
The Lairds Most Likely Book 10

Young love torn apart.

As teenagers, Malcolm Innes and Rhona Macleod fell passionately in love. But Malcom's parents were horrified to think of the aristocratic heir to Dun Carron marrying a humble crofter's daughter. Desperate to crush the affair, they locked Malcolm up and exiled Rhona to London where she disappears. But Malcolm is faithful and stubborn and devotes his life to searching for his beloved and the child she was carrying when they were cruelly separated.

A chance to mend two shattered lives.

On a snowy Christmas Eve, Rhona opens the door of her isolated farmhouse to find the man she never thought to see again, the man who betrayed her. When she was pregnant with his son, Malcolm abandoned her to find her way alone in a cold, heartless world. Now she discovers that her long-held hatred is based on lies and that he's been true to her. Yet surely after all these years, it's too late to awaken the love that once united them.

As Christmas Eve turns into Christmas Day, Malcolm and Rhona discover that their mutual desire has never died. Will this Yuletide reunion lead to a lifetime together? Or has old tragedy ruptured their bond forever?

www.ingramcontent.com/pod-product-compliance
Lightning Source LLC
Chambersburg PA
CBHW030800190726
48285CB00003B/951